TOBY BELFER
Learns about Heroes and Martyrs

TOBY BELFER
Learns about Heroes and Martyrs

By Gloria Teles Pushker and Mel Tarman
Illustrated by Emile Henriquez

PELICAN PUBLISHING COMPANY
GRETNA 2009

*The word "Pelican" and the depiction of a pelican are trademarks
of Pelican Publishing Company, Inc., and are registered in the
U.S. Patent and Trademark Office.*

Library of Congress Cataloging-in-Publication Data

Pushker, Gloria Teles.
  Toby Belfer learns about heroes and martyrs / by Gloria Teles Pushker
and Mel Tarman ; illustrated by Emile Henriquez.
     p. cm.
  Includes bibliographical references.
  ISBN 978-1-58980-647-4 (hardcover : alk. paper) 1. Righteous Gentiles
in the Holocaust—Juvenile literature. 2. Righteous Gentiles in the
Holocaust—Biography—Juvenile literature. 3. Holocaust, Jewish (1939-
1945)—Juvenile literature. 4. Yad va-shem, rashut ha-zikaron la-Sho'ah
vela-gevurah—Juvenile literature. 5. Heroes—Europe—Biography—
Juvenile literature. 6. Martyrs—Europe—Biography—Juvenile literature.
7. World War, 1939-1945—Jews—Rescue—Juvenile literature. 8. World
War, 1939-1945—Jewish resistance—Juvenile literature. I. Tarman, Mel.
II. Henriquez, Emile F., ill. III. Title.
  D804.65.P87 2009
  940.53'1835—dc22

                                    2008050365

Printed in the United States of America
Published by Pelican Publishing Company, Inc.
1000 Burmaster Street, Gretna, Louisiana 70053

*To my grandson, Adam Jacob, who filmed Yad Vashem, and
to Phil Gaethe, education director of Congregation
Gates of Prayer, Metairie, Louisiana—G. T. P.*

*To my grandchildren, Elise and Adam Black and Leo Samuel Tarman,
who I hope will grow up to be righteous persons, and to the 6 million Jews
killed in the Holocaust and the Righteous Gentiles who saved so many
—M. T.*

*To Linda Hooper, principal of Whitwell Middle School,
Whitwell, Tennessee, and the students and residents of this community
who participated in the "Paper Clip Project"—G. T. P. and M. T.*

He who saves one human life is as he saves the entire world.

Talmud

The honors given to the "just gentiles" by the State of Israel at Yad Vashem for having acting heroically to save Jews, sometimes to the point of giving their own lives, is a recognition that not even in the darkest hour is every light extinguished . . . evil will not have the last word.

Pope John Paul II at Yad Vashem, March 23, 2000

Contents

Preface

Jews have lived in Europe for centuries. Many of them were poor farmers; some were merchants, bankers, lawyers, doctors, teachers, scientists, writers, and musicians. They all played an important part in the cultural life of each country they lived in, but they suffered persecution in most of those countries. Some countries disliked Jews more than other countries did. When Adolf Hitler became leader of Germany during the 1930s, the Jews there suffered the most.

Hitler hated the Jews for no reason other than that they were Jews. The German Jews contributed greatly to German society. Many were doctors, teachers, scientists, and business leaders. Some were even high-ranking military officers or politicians. Hitler thought the Jews were an inferior race, even though Judaism is not a race, it is a religion like Christianity. He began the persecution of Jews by barring them from teaching, holding political office, and practicing medicine. Their stores were vandalized, their synagogues destroyed, and their holy books burned. They were beaten and humiliated in the street and, in many cases, arrested and imprisoned for no reason.

When Hitler's army invaded Poland in 1939 and started World War II, his reign of terror against Jews spread to all countries he occupied: Denmark, Norway, Holland, Belgium, France, Yugoslavia, Hungary, Czechoslovakia, Latvia, Italy, and Greece. Jews under the Nazi occupiers were forced to wear yellow stars on their clothing to identify them as Jews. They were herded into areas in their own cities called ghettos, where they had to live separately from the rest of the population. Many died from starvation or disease. Those who tried to escape were either shot or imprisoned in concentration camps.

Soon the Jews in each of those countries were rounded up and sent to railroad stations to await deportation to these camps. Men, women, and children were sent away and 6 million Jews died in the camps. Along with the Jews were many Catholic priests and nuns, gypsies, and other people whom Hitler considered undesirable or who did not agree with his policies. As this horrible slaughter, now known as the Holocaust, was taking place, many people were silent and did not protest. However, there were some courageous Christians, or "gentiles," who saw this inhumane treatment of Jews and risked their lives to hide them, feed them, or help them escape to friendly countries. Some of the Jews they helped were friends and neighbors; some were complete strangers.

These Christians saved thousands of Jewish lives. Over twenty thousand of these brave men and women from various countries are honored as "Righteous Gentiles" by the State of Israel at Yad Vashem, the Museum for the Remembrance of Holocaust Martyrs and Heroes in Jerusalem. "Righteous" means that they acted in an upright, moral way. There are many names and stories of good Christians that may never be known, but they will all be honored by God. The Holocaust showed the world the worst of mankind, but in these cases it also showed the best.

In this book, Toby Belfer, our fifth grader, tells the story of some of those Righteous Gentiles and what they did to help their fellow human beings. These and the unknown gentiles are true heroes, who will be remembered in history forever. Toby and her Christian friend, Donna, also tell about their visit to Whitwell, Tennessee, the home of the "Paper Clip Project." This book is an attempt to educate children about an important event in history, with the hope that it will never happen again.

TOBY BELFER
Learns about Heroes and Martyrs

PART 1

Yad Vashem:
The Holocaust History Museum
in Jerusalem

CHAPTER 1

Toby Learns about "Righteous Gentiles"

The April sky was a deep blue and the sunlight bounced off the golden Dome of the Rock in the holy city of Jerusalem. Toby Belfer and her best friend, Donna Barker, awoke early in their small hotel room. "I can't believe this is our last day in Israel," Toby said sadly to Donna. The girls were on spring break with their fifth-grade history class from Louisiana, and they had spent a glorious week touring the Holy Land and meeting people from different cultures. Now it was almost time to return home, but first Toby and her classmates were going to pay their respects at Yad Vashem, the Museum for the Remembrance of Holocaust Martyrs and Heroes. Today was a particularly meaningful day in Israel. It was Yom Hashoah, the day of remembrance for the 6 million Jews killed by the Nazis during World War II.

As the bus wound its way through the narrow streets of Jerusalem towards the museum, a siren wailed and the bus came to a dead stop. "Every year on this day, a siren sounds at precisely ten o'clock and the entire country comes to a standstill," said Avi, the bus driver. "Traffic stops and people get out of their cars or buses. Pedestrians stop walking and everyone observes two minutes of silence in memory of the 6 million Jews who died in the Holocaust," he explained to the children. All of the children got off the bus and stood in silence for two minutes until the siren wailed again, signaling the end of the silent devotion.

Back on the bus, Avi went on, "This is a solemn day in Israel as well as in Jewish communities throughout the world. Here in Israel, all theaters are closed today, many restaurants are also closed, and no public events take place."

The bus began its journey again. When the museum finally came into view in the western outskirts of Jerusalem, Donna exclaimed, "My goodness, what a beautiful building! It's built into the side of a mountain." The ridge is known as the Mount of Remembrance.

"I have never seen anything like this," Toby said in awe. "Look how the big skylight lets the sun shine on the different parts of the building. It's as if God is shining a holy light on the museum. How neat!"

When the class got off the bus, they first went into the Hall of Names, which contains the records of individuals who died in the Holocaust. Toby and Donna carefully studied the stories and pictures of men, women, and children who were imprisoned and killed by the Nazis in the various concentration camps. Some were Toby and Donna's age. Many were younger. Next, the class moved into the large art gallery, where they saw the lovely artwork done by the victims. There were colorful paintings of flowers and butterflies by children who had proudly signed their names. The art seemed to express hope and freedom.

After viewing the paintings, they all silently filed into the Hall of Remembrance. It was totally dark except for five candles that shone brightly in mirrors that surrounded the hall. The reflections in the mirrors made it seem as if 150,000 candles were lit, one for each child who died. An eternal flame also burned, surrounded by stones that were set into the floor and inscribed with names such as Auschwitz, Dachau, Buchenwald, and Treblinka. Toby silently read them. "Those were some of the terrible places where the Nazis sent Jews and other people they hated," she whispered to Donna. As she continued reading the names, Toby thought about her friends and family back home and gave thanks that she lived in America, a land of freedom for all races and religions. She knew that she could worship in her synagogue, go to school, go to the library, and read whatever she wanted. She could go shopping with her friends and parents without being afraid. Yes, she was grateful to be an American and live in such a wonderful land.

Tears filled her eyes as she and the other Jewish visitors recited the *Kaddish,* the Jewish prayer for the dead. Her Christian friend Donna, along with other gentile visitors, prayed according to their own faith. Some fingered rosaries as they recited their prayers; some chanted the Lord's Prayer. Toby even heard a pastor from Georgia leading his group in the Twenty-third Psalm. There were people from different countries and religions all paying their respects to these martyrs in the Hall of Remembrance. It was a very moving moment for Toby and all the visitors.

As the class left the hall and walked back into the sunshine, everyone was deep in thought. Not a sound could be heard among them. Toby noticed an old railroad car in the center of the memorial site. "Oh, look, Donna. This must have been one of those cars used to transport the Jews and others to the concentration camps."

"How awful it must have been," replied her friend. The car was an original cattle car given to Yad Vashem by the Polish government. It stands on a small slope facing the hills of Jerusalem. The car serves as a symbol of the horror of the Holocaust but also conveys hope and the gift of life.

They approached the Avenue of the Righteous Among the Nations. Toby saw thousands of trees lining the pathways, each with a marker. Those trees were planted to honor the brave Christian men and women, called "Righteous Gentiles," who risked their own lives trying to save Jews. Each tree was marked with the name of a hero who was honored by the State of Israel. There were also "walls of honor" with nearly twenty thousand names engraved on plaques. As Toby read the names on the walls, she said to Donna, "Look, there are French names, Danish and Swedish names, Dutch names, Italian names, Polish and Russian names—even German names." There were some names Toby couldn't pronounce, but in her heart she knew they were all heroes.

Toby and Donna returned to the avenue to read some of the markers on the trees. Toby saw one for a Franciscan monk and one for a Greek bishop. She saw the names of a Polish nun and a Protestant minister. Donna said, "Look, Toby, here is one for Pierre Marie Benoit, a Catholic priest who with the approval of the Vatican helped many victims escape to Spain and Switzerland, both friendly countries. My teacher told me about him in my Sunday-school class."

Toby wasn't surprised to see a tree planted in honor of Raoul Wallenberg, the Swedish diplomat who saved thousands of Hungarian Jews. She knew about his bravery from her teachers. She even saw streets named after him in Israel. Then she saw Oskar Schindler's tree. He was the brave German who hired many Jewish people to work in his factory so they wouldn't be sent to concentration camps. He protected, as he called them, "my Jewish children." "I saw a movie about him not long ago called *Schindler's List*," Toby said. "But what's this Japanese name on a tree, Senpo Sugihara?" she asked her teacher, Mrs. Miller. "Weren't Germany and Japan at war with America at that time?"

"This Japanese diplomat in Lithuania was a brave hero who

defied his government's orders and issued visas for Jews to head to safe countries," Mrs. Miller answered. "He saved thousands of lives."

Toby was surprised to see all these names and wanted to learn more about what those people did to be so honored. She asked Mrs. Miller if she and Donna could go back into the Hall of Names and read some of the stories of these Righteous Gentiles. "Of course," replied Mrs. Miller. "See if you can place the names with the ones you just saw on the trees or the walls and read their stories. Then we can discuss their deeds with the entire class when we return home."

Toby was eager to start this project. She and Donna returned to the Hall of Names and started to read and write down some of the stories of these brave people so others could learn the lessons of the Holocaust.

PART 2

Extraordinary People

CHAPTER 2

Corrie ten Boom

Corrie ten Boom was a devout Christian. She and her family belonged to the Dutch Reformed Church, and it was her strong faith that enabled her to survive her terrible ordeal.

Corrie's mother died when Corrie was very young. She and sister Betsie lived with their father. A jeweler and watchmaker, he had a little shop in Amsterdam. He trained Corrie in watch making, and when she was twenty, she worked with him in the shop. Many of their customers were Jewish and Corrie came to know them and their families. She made friends with them and even joined them in their homes Friday evenings to celebrate the Jewish Sabbath. Together, she and her Jewish friends studied the Old Testament and the Jewish prophets. She loved spending time with her friends.

When the Germans invaded Holland in 1940, the little country had no choice but to surrender to their mighty army. Otherwise, it would have been completely destroyed. Everyone was issued ration cards to buy food. All newspapers were shut down and all radios had to be turned in to the German authorities. No one was allowed on the streets after six o'clock in the evening. Jews in particular suffered greatly. Many of their homes were broken into by the Germans and their valuables stolen. Their places of worship were vandalized, and they were often beaten on the street for no apparent reason. All Jewish men, women, and children were made to sew a yellow star on their clothing in order to identify them as Jews. This was meant to humiliate them and set them apart from the rest of the population.

Corrie and her father were very disturbed by this persecution of the Jews. So many of her good friends were Jewish. They loved and respected one another. One horrible Sunday afternoon, German soldiers began taking all Jewish boys from their parents, to be sent to Germany to work in their factories. Most of these children were never seen or heard from again, for when they were too weak from starvation to work any longer, they were sent away to concentration camps and eventually died.

Corrie knew she must do something to save the remaining boys and shelter her friends. She built a false wall in her house, behind which she hid many Jews who were forced out of their own homes. At one time she had seven Jews hiding in the cramped quarters behind the wall. Corrie persuaded some of her Christian friends and neighbors to hide as many Jews as they could. She distributed hundreds of stolen ration cards to her friends to help feed the Jews they were sheltering.

One day a man that Corrie knew came into her shop and told her that he too was hiding Jews but needed money. He made up a lie that his wife was arrested by the Nazis and he needed the money to bribe the guards to let her out of prison. Corrie was sympathetic to his story and promised to help him. She didn't know that this man was actually an informant who was sent to trick her. He promptly reported to the Germans that Corrie was hiding and feeding Jews.

The Nazis raided her home and arrested her and her family. Fortunately, the Jews she was hiding managed to escape, but not Corrie. She, her father, and her sister were sent to a concentration camp. They slept on a bare floor in a cold cell. They had no blankets or warm clothing. Her father became sick and died a few weeks after they were arrested. Betsie also became ill and died shortly thereafter.

While Corrie was in prison, she held secret religious services for people of all faiths. Roman Catholics attended, as well as Lutherans, Eastern Orthodox Christians, and even Jews. The prisoners in the camp were from many different countries, such as the Netherlands (Holland), France, Poland, Czechoslovakia, and the Soviet Union. Corrie gave them hope as they prayed together. It didn't matter what religion they were. They all prayed to God.

Corrie ten Boom was released from prison because of a clerical error by the Nazis. She felt that God had intervened on her behalf. She was very lucky, because she learned that all the women in the prison were killed. She was terribly weak and sick and had to nurse herself back to health. When the war ended, she set up a home for concentration-camp survivors so that they could heal both physically and mentally. She fed them, tended to the sick, and held religious services. All faiths were welcomed into her home, no questions asked. Most of the survivors were Jewish.

After a while, Corrie decided to travel around the world preaching and telling all who would listen about what she learned during those terrible years of fear and imprisonment. She knew in her heart that she was saved by God to share her story. After many years of traveling and preaching, she retired and moved to California. She died at the age of ninety-one.

The story of this heroic Dutch woman was made into a movie called *The Hiding Place.* It was seen by millions of people. Her home where she hid the Jews was turned into a museum. The queen of the Netherlands recognized her bravery and knighted her. In 1987 Corrie ten Bloom was declared "Righteous Among the Nations" by the State of Israel. A tree is planted in her honor at Yad Vashem.

CHAPTER 3

Janis Lipke

Janis Lipke was living in Latvia, a part of the Soviet Union, when the Germans arrived as occupiers in 1941. When he saw the brutal massacre of Jews in the capital city of Riga, he vowed to do everything he possibly could to save them from the Germans. Many Latvians were friendly towards the occupiers and worked with them in persecuting Jews, so Lipke knew the risk he was taking.

Janis was a dockworker, but when the Germans occupied his country he joined the German air force, known as the *Luftwaffe*, as a civilian worker. The pay was better than his old job. Since he was part of the German military now, he was able to enter the ghetto where the Jews were forced to live. He devised a very clever plan. Each day, he brought out several Jews to work as laborers for the German air force. Then each evening, his trusted friends would put on the identification badges that all Jews were forced to wear and go inside the ghetto, impersonating the Jews that Janis had brought out that day. When the Germans counted everyone who returned, no one seemed to be missing. In the morning these same men would come out with new Jewish laborers. These Jews then simply gave their badges to a new group of friends, who would go into the ghetto that evening. The Germans didn't seem to catch on to this game, but it was very risky for everyone because these men, along with the Jews, would have been shot if the plot was discovered.

As the Jews were brought out each day, they were given some money that Lipke borrowed from friends and relatives. He then helped coordinate their escape. Sometimes he had to bribe the German border guards to look the other way. He also took several Jews to his own home and hid them beneath piles of lumber in his yard. Lipke's wife, Johanna, and his eldest son encouraged him and helped bring food to the Jews in hiding.

Lipke knew he couldn't hide these Jews forever, so with his experience as a dockworker, he prepared a boat to take them to Sweden, which was a safe country. However, the Germans learned about the plan from an informer. Lipke was arrested and imprisoned. Luckily, some of his contacts in the German air force vouched for him, and he was released with a stern warning. Otherwise, he surely would have been shot for his illegal activities.

This setback did not stop this brave man. He was determined to continue helping Jews. Using his meager savings, he bought a small farm on the outskirts of Riga and used it to hide those Jews who were able to escape from the ghetto.

He fed them and sheltered them until his network of sympathetic friends could smuggle them out of the country to safe locations. If not for Lipke's efforts, these Jews would surely have been sent to concentration camps and certain death.

From 1941 to 1944, Lipke continued his humanitarian work. He and his wife knew the risks they were taking but felt it was their duty to help these unfortunate people. This Righteous Gentile saved hundreds of Jews. When the Soviet army finally drove the Nazis out of Latvia, Janis Lipke was able to discontinue these activities and return to a normal life.

In 1966, the State of Israel formally honored Janis and Johanna Lipke at Yad Vashem as "Righteous Among the Nations."

CHAPTER 4

Alex and Mela Roslan

Alex and Mela lived in a small village in Poland called Bialystock ("Bee-*ah*-lee-stock"). Alex's father was a shoemaker, and most of his customers were poor Jewish farmers or shopkeepers. Although Alex's father was not a very religious man, he knew right from wrong and didn't cheat his customers. He taught his son these same values and told him to always fight for truth and justice. Alex married Mela in 1928. A son was born three years later and a daughter soon followed. Alex made a decent living as a textile merchant, and many of his customers were the same Jewish customers who frequented his father's shop. They liked and respected one another.

When the Germans occupied Poland, they forced all the Jews to live in ghettos. Alex wondered where all his customers were. He learned that they were all living in the ghetto, which was separated from the rest of the city by a wall. He asked a friend to help him get into the ghetto. Together they dug a tunnel under the wall and were able to sneak into the ghetto at night. What he saw horrified him. There were so many sickly children begging for food that he knew he had to help. When he returned home, he told Mela that he was going to smuggle a child out of the ghetto and bring him home. He said even if he saved only one child, he would be doing God's work. The next night, Alex smuggled a boy named Jacob out of the ghetto and brought him home with him. This was very dangerous, because if they were caught they would both be shot. Alex told Jacob that from now on his name would be Genek, a good Polish name. If anyone should ask or become suspicious, he should pretend to be Christian, but Alex told him to remember that in his heart he would always be Jewish. He told the boy to remember his faith.

The Roslan family built a false floor under their kitchen and that's where Jacob hid. Alex's son and daughter would share their small ration of food with Jacob. They would tell him stories, play games with him, and try to keep his spirits up. Jacob was lonely and

frightened. A few weeks later, the German secret police, called the Gestapo, received a tip and came to search Alex's house.

They were looking for Jewish children who escaped from the ghetto. Everyone in the house was frightened as they searched and searched but came up empty handed. They were standing on the very floor under which Jacob was hiding. Alex knew he would have to move away because someone was already suspicious enough to contact the Gestapo. He found a larger house with more space.

Instead of hiding Jacob under the floor, he hid him in the false bottom of a large couch he built in his shop. Now that Alex had more room in his house, he wanted to smuggle more children out of the ghetto. Mela was afraid to take another Jewish child. Alex convinced her that it was the right thing to do. After all, it wouldn't matter if they were caught with one, two, or three children. They would be shot anyway. Alex smuggled another boy named Sholom out of the ghetto and changed his name to Orish. This young boy was very sick and weak. Mela tried to nurse him back to health. They gave him food from their own rations. Alex's two children would go up to the attic where Orish was hiding and play with him, but Orish was so weak he could hardly stand up. The young Jewish boy died in the attic a few weeks later. Alex and Mela were very sad that they couldn't save him, but they knew they did everything they could to make him comfortable his last few weeks. At least he didn't die on the street.

When the war ended, Alex's business prospered again. He and Mela adopted Jacob as their own child because his parents died in the ghetto. Alex told him again that he was to remain true to his Jewish faith. This good Christian family risked their lives trying to save Jewish children, and for that the State of Israel honored Alex and Mela Roslan as "Righteous Among the Nations."

CHAPTER 5

Tamara Maximenoc-Bromberg

Unlike most of the people in her hometown of Odessa in the Ukraine, Tamara Maximenoc and her mother were very sympathetic to the Jews of their country, who, under the German occupation, were forced to live in ghettos. Tamara knew the horrible conditions the Jews endured there, so she would sneak into the ghetto at night and bring food and warm clothing to the starving children. Many times she and her mother would bribe German guards with jewelry to let them in and out of the ghetto. One night, as they were about to leave the ghetto, they were stopped at the gate. This wasn't the same guard they had bribed earlier. Tamara and her mother were forced to live in the ghetto for over a week. They suffered terribly from the cold and hunger, just like the Jews.

Tamara's mother was of Greek extraction and knew how to speak the language. By speaking Greek to the Germans, she was able to convince them that they were not Jewish and did not belong in the ghetto. After all, the Germans thought, no Jew was smart enough to speak Greek, so they must be telling the truth. They were released. Having experienced the horrible day-to-day conditions of the ghetto, Tamara was now more resolved than ever to do everything she could to help these poor people survive.

She continued to sneak into the ghetto at night, knowing that if she was ever caught, she couldn't talk her way out again and she would be sent to prison. There were signs posted everywhere warning against helping Jews. Tamara was able to smuggle a Jewish family of four out of the ghetto and hide them in her house. She knew she had to help them escape to another country, so she bribed the border guards with the rest of her jewelry and they let the family of Jews pass.

When the war ended, Tamara continued her humanitarian work. Jews who had survived the ghetto had no place to go. Those who did not die from starvation or disease were left homeless. Tamara helped them rebuild their lives by finding them places to live. She was even able to get them jobs.

Many of her neighbors openly scorned her and called her a "Jew lover." Odessa was a very anti-Semitic town. No one knows how many Jews would have died if not for this good Christian woman's courage. She and her mother risked their lives to help strangers in need.

Because she was shunned by her neighbors, Tamara and her mother moved to Israel to start a new life. She met and married a Jewish businessman by the name of Bromberg. The family she hid in her house during the war wrote to Yad Vashem about how Tamara saved many Jewish lives. Israel recognized her heroism and sacrifice during the war, and Tamara Maximenoc-Bromberg was granted full Israeli citizenship and honored as "Righteous Among the Nations."

CHAPTER 6

Miep Gies

If not for Miep Gies ("Meep Gheess"), the world would never have met and embraced Anne Frank. Miep was the brave woman who helped the Frank family survive for several years during the German occupation of Amsterdam, Holland.

For more than two years, Gies risked her own life to protect and care for the Franks and four of their friends in their secret hiding place. There were many other brave Dutch families who sheltered Jews during the war, but she became known because she hid Anne Frank. Gies never claimed to be a hero. She always maintained that Anne and her family were the true heroes.

Miep Gies was born in Vienna, Austria. She was a frail child and contracted tuberculosis. Her family sent her to live with foster parents in Amsterdam because they thought the air was cleaner and it would be healthier for their daughter. Her new foster parents welcomed her and shared everything they had with her, treating Miep as one of their own children. The love that she experienced from them so impressed her that, when she grew up, she decided to make Holland her permanent home. The kindness and humanitarian values she learned from her new parents influenced her actions in later life.

Miep worked in the office of a Jewish businessman, Otto Frank. When the Nazis began their terrible persecution of Jews in Holland, Mr. Frank asked Gies if she would help hide him and his family. Without hesitation, she said yes. She felt it her duty to help anyone in trouble. The Franks had been kind to her and treated her like family. Mr. Frank built a secret annex to his office, where he, his wife, their daughters, Margot and Anne, and four friends hid for years. Miep provided them with food, clothing, and books. Even though she knew she was taking a great risk, she acted because of the great moral values instilled in her by her loving foster parents. She was the Franks' only hope for surviving the war.

It is not fully known who finally betrayed the Franks and their

secret annex. It is generally thought that a neighbor became suspicious when the Franks disappeared and reported these suspicions to the Gestapo. The secret annex was discovered and the Franks were taken away to a concentration camp. Even then, Miep tried to bribe the German officer who arrested them. She then went to Nazi headquarters to work out a deal to spare their lives, aware that this move could cost her own life. Unfortunately, she was unsuccessful in getting the Franks released.

Miep had hope that Anne and her family would return after the war. She went back to the office to clean up the annex where the Franks hid all those years. She found many of Anne's notes scattered about. She collected them and waited for the family's return.

Mr. Frank did survive imprisonment and returned to his office, but Miep learned that Anne Frank died in Bergen-Belsen concentration camp from a terrible disease called typhus. She was fifteen years old. Her sister, Margot, had died earlier from the same disease. Ever since the day that Mr. Frank gave Miep this sad news about Anne and her sister, she has mourned the cruel fate of her Jewish friends.

When Mr. Frank returned to the annex, he collected all of the papers Miep found, as well as a diary Anne had written from June 1942 until her capture in August 1944. In the diary, Anne outlined her daily activities, but she also wrote of hope, faith, and optimism about the world and the future. The diary was published in 1947 and is one of the most widely read books in history. *The Diary of a Young Girl* has been translated into fifty-five languages and is recognized for its historical value as a document of the Holocaust as well as for the high quality of writing displayed by so young an author. The house where the Franks hid has become a national museum, and thousands of tourists visit each year. There are dozens of Anne Frank educational societies throughout the world. Anne has become a symbol of light and hope during one of the darkest periods in history.

Miep Gies has been honored throughout the world for her bravery. She risked her life to shelter her Jewish friends, kept them alive for several years, and gave them hope. The State of Israel has paid tribute to this fine Christian woman at Yad Vashem as "Righteous Among the Nations."

CHAPTER 7

Jadwiga Suchodolski

One evening in April 1943, the Suchodolski ("Soo-co-*dahl*-skee") family heard a faint knock on their door. When they opened it, they found their former neighbor, obviously starving, pleading with them to hide him from the Nazis.

Adam Suchodolski, his wife, Stanislawa, and their teenage daughter, Jadwiga ("*Yad*-wig-uh"), lived in a small village on the outskirts of Warsaw, the capital of Poland. They were devout Catholics, like most of their neighbors. They believed in Jesus and tried to obey the Ten Commandments. After hastily consulting among themselves, the family decided to take in and shelter their former neighbor, a Jewish lawyer named Michael Shaft.

Michael Shaft had left the village several years before, as a young man. He went to live and study law in Warsaw. When the Germans invaded Poland, the Jews in the city were all rounded up and forced to live in a ghetto. It was surrounded by a wall and guarded by soldiers so no Jew could escape.

After living for many years in the ghetto under terrible conditions, the Jews rebelled in April 1943. This is known in history as the Warsaw ghetto uprising. The Germans brought in their army to quell the rebellion. Heavy fighting followed. The Germans had tanks and artillery. The Jews had a few guns that they managed to smuggle in and some homemade bombs. But they also had determination. After a month, the Germans with their superior army were able to crush the rebellion, but they lost many men and much equipment to the brave Jewish resistance fighters. All the remaining Jews were rounded up. Many of them were shot; the rest were sent away to concentration camps. Michael participated in the Warsaw ghetto uprising but managed to escape before the roundup. He hid in the woods for several days and eventually made his way back to his native village, where he thought he might be safe.

The Suchodolskis heard rumors of the uprising in Warsaw. When Michael told them he escaped and needed a place to hide, they agreed to shelter him. This was a very dangerous decision, because their friends and neighbors were unfriendly towards the Jews and very untrustworthy. Most of them were glad that the Jews were put in a ghetto, and they didn't really care what happened to them. Knowing the risks they were taking, the Suchodolski family decided to keep their friend safe from the Germans.

They dug a pit under their barn and covered it with hay. Michael hid in that narrow pit for almost two years. Jadwiga provided him with food through a small opening. In the winter, rain and snow leaked into the pit In the summer, the heat was unbearable. Despite all of these discomforts, Michael was thankful that he was safe from the Germans in this cramped hiding place under the barn.

Poland was finally liberated by the Soviets in January 1945. Now Suchodolski could free his friend from his hiding place. The family took Michael into their home to feed him and try and restore his health. Word spread that a Jew had been hidden in the village. A large group of angry Poles stormed the Suchodolskis' home. They knew that if the Nazis had found out about the Jew hiding there, the entire village would have been punished. They demanded that the Jew be turned over to them. The Suchodolskis resisted long enough for Michael to escape through the back door. When the mob couldn't find the Jew, they ransacked the house in revenge and threatened the family, calling them "Jew lovers." The family was shunned by the village. Several days later, Michael was able to sneak back and thank this wonderful Christian family for saving his life.

Michael spent some more time with the Suchodolskis until he was strong and healthy. They weren't afraid of the villagers and kept him in their house as long as he wanted to stay. The young lawyer and Jadwiga fell in love and emigrated to Israel, where they were married and started a new life together. In 1972, Jadwiga was honored by the State of Israel as "Righteous Among the Nations." She accepted this high honor on behalf of the entire Suchodolski family. She said her family wasn't afraid of their anti-Semitic neighbors and only did what God would want them to do.

CHAPTER 8

Irena Sendler

At least twenty-five hundred Jewish children owe their lives to this courageous Polish woman who came from a small village near Warsaw. Her father was a gentle country doctor whose patients were mostly poor Jewish farmers. Dr. Sendler's compassion had a great influence on his daughter, Irena, as she grew up.

Irena was a health worker in the Warsaw social welfare department. Her department provided meals, money, and medicine to poor Polish citizens. Under the German occupation of Poland, Jews were forced to live behind the walls of the ghetto. Their Polish neighbors mostly turned their backs on them, and over five thousand Warsaw Jews a month died from starvation or disease. Irena Sendler did not turn her back. Her position in the welfare department enabled her to smuggle food, medicine, and warm clothing into the ghetto. Defying the Nazis, she also arranged to smuggle Jewish children out of the ghetto. First she had to find sympathetic Polish families to adopt them and pretend they were their own children. This was no easy task, for there weren't many families willing to risk their lives for Jews. Then she had to persuade families in the ghetto to give up their children for adoption. This was the only way to save these children's lives.

Irena began smuggling the children out of the ghetto in an ambulance. Sometimes she had to use large flour sacks or garbage bags to get these children out. Other times she buried the children in a truck under great piles of food. She used any means she could to smuggle them out, because she knew they would surely die if she didn't help them.

Irena then forged documents for each child, claiming they had been baptized as Christians. The Catholic Church also helped her. Many of the children were sent to religious establishments, where Irena knew the nuns would take good care of them. Few nuns refused to help this determined woman save her children.

In order to keep a record of the children she rescued, Irena

placed their original Jewish names along with their fake Christian names in jars. She also recorded the home or convent where each child was sent. She did this in code, so only she knew the true identities of the children. She buried the jars beneath a tree in a friendly neighbor's yard. One day she knew she would dig up the jars, try to locate these children, and give them back their true identities. The jars held the names of 2,500 children she managed to smuggle out of the Warsaw ghetto and save.

The Nazis became aware of Irena's illegal activities and she was arrested and imprisoned. During her imprisonment she was beaten repeatedly. The Nazis wanted to know where she hid the children. Irena never told where they were or where her jars with their names were buried. She was sentenced to death, but one of the Polish guards who knew Irena and her father helped her escape and Irena went into hiding. The Germans searched and searched but could never find her.

When the war ended and Irena came out of hiding, she hurried to her neighbor's yard where the jars were buried. She quickly dug them up and removed the names. She began her search for the children she saved in order to reunite them with their real families. Unfortunately, most of them died in the ghetto or concentration camps. Very few of the children were able to see their parents again.

Irena Sendler's heroic deeds were not known for years. The true story of this courageous lady was uncovered by four young students in a Kansas high school. They learned about her from a newspaper article and were so impressed by her bravery that they wrote a play for a history competition. The play, named *Life in a Jar,* introduced the world to this Polish hero.

In 1965, Irena Sendler was made an honorary citizen of Israel and named "Righteous Among the Nations."

CHAPTER 9

Jozef Zwonarz

Toby and Donna read a story of a most amazing man, one who risked everything he had to hide a Jewish couple. Even his wife and five children did not learn of his good deed until later on. He was afraid that they might say something by mistake to someone unfriendly towards the Jews. What is even more amazing is that his little house where he sheltered the Jews was in the middle of German and Ukrainian police headquarters in the little town of Lesko in the Ukraine.

A Jewish doctor learned from some friends that the Germans were planning to send all of the Jewish children in town to concentration camps. The doctor's wife knew Jozef Zwonarz ("*Zwon*-arts"), an iron maker, to be a compassionate man who was opposed to the persecution of the Jews, so she immediately contacted him for help. Jozef asked a good friend to hide her child. When the wife learned that the Jewish women were also going to be sent away by the Germans, she again appealed to Jozef for help. Without hesitation, he promised to hide her and her husband. He built a shelter beneath his workshop, which was close to his home. The doctor and his wife hid in these cramped quarters. Jozef fed them bread and potatoes from his small rations. Sometimes he took his entire dinner to them, going without food himself. The hiding place was so small that the doctor and his wife could not stand or even sit up. They had to lie down in the shelter all the time. That's how they survived for two years. They couldn't go outside, for they were hiding in the middle of the town and they were afraid someone might spot them and notify the police.

Jozef needed money to feed them, but the doctor could not pay him for his generosity. So Jozef had to take an extra job as a farmhand. Many times he was paid with just a sack of barley, which he promptly gave to the doctor and his wife. He set up a small stove in the hiding place and they were able to cook the barley. Zwonarz visited them every night to see that they were all right. Jozef's wife finally became suspicious of his strange activities. She confronted him and he had to lie to her. He did not want to involve his wife. It was too dangerous.

The Soviet army was approaching Lesko and started to bomb the town. A shell struck the underground shelter and Jozef had to move the doctor and his wife to the cellar of his house. Since they were lying down for almost two years, their leg muscles were too weak for them to stand and they had to crawl to the house. The sunlight nearly blinded them. Now Jozef had no choice but to tell his wife of his illegal activities. She was not surprised that this good man would do this and she agreed to help him hide the Jews in their cellar. The doctor and his wife hid there for six weeks before the Soviet army liberated the town. During that time, Jozef fed them and helped them regain their strength and the use of their legs. When they were able to leave the house, they were reunited with their little daughter. They felt ashamed that they could not repay the kindness of this Ukrainian farmer and his wife. Jozef said he didn't want any money. In fact, he gave some money to them to start a new life.

Many of Zwonarz's neighbors made ugly remarks to him when they learned that he had hidden the Jewish couple. Most of the townspeople were very anti-Semitic. Jozef merely responded that he did what everyone in the town should have done. He was ashamed of his neighbors.

The Jewish doctor and his family rebuilt their lives thanks to this heroic man. He risked everything for them. He and his entire family would have been sent to a concentration camp if they were caught by the Germans or the Ukrainian police. For his heroism and compassion, the State of Israel honored Jozef Zwonarz at Yad Vashem as "Righteous Among the Nations."

"I think this is the region where my grandparents grew up before they came to America," Toby said after reading about this Righteous Gentile. "I'll have to ask Mama. I'm sure glad they decided to leave."

CHAPTER 10

The Kozminski Family

The Glazer family was Jewish and the Kozminski family was Catholic, but they were good friends in Warsaw, the capital of Poland. When the Germans occupied that city, the Glazers, like all the Jewish families in Warsaw, were forced to live in the ghetto. No one could escape the walled and guarded ghetto, and non-Jews had to have a special pass to enter.

Jerzy was the seventeen-year-old son in the Kozminski family. He, like his entire family, was upset at the terrible persecution of the Jews in Warsaw. Many were neighbors and friends of the family, especially the Glazers. Jerzy would sneak into the ghetto at night and smuggle food and clothing to them. One evening he was in the ghetto past curfew time. Everyone had to be in their houses at curfew or they would be imprisoned. Jerzy had to hide and sleep in the Glazers' home. The following day, April 19, 1943, the Jews in the ghetto rebelled against the German occupiers. There was heavy fighting on both sides and Samuel Glazer felt terrible that this young man was caught in the middle of the uprising. He told Jerzy to escape and go home. Before Jerzy left, he told Samuel to come hide with his own family if he escaped.

Most of the Jews were killed in the fighting. The remainder were rounded up and either shot or sent to concentration camps and eventual death. A few lucky ones managed to escape during the chaotic weeks of fighting. Among them were Samuel Glazer, his wife, his father, and nine additional relatives. Glazer remembered Jerzy's promise of shelter should he escape the ghetto. When they appeared at the Kozminski house, Mr. Kozminski was afraid that such a large group, twelve in all, would be very dangerous to hide.

Teresa, Mr. Kozminski's wife, insisted that they all remain together. Mr. Kozminiski built a shelter for them under the wooden floor of his house. The Glazers hid here for sixteen months. Samuel paid for their upkeep from the small amount of money and family jewels he was able to smuggle out of the ghetto.

When his money ran out, the Kozminskis continued to care for them. Word spread about the Kozminski family to other Jews who had managed to escape the ghetto, and they all knocked on their door. Soon the crowded shelter was hiding twenty-two. The Kozminskis cared for them all. One day as young Jerzy was out scavenging for food, he was arrested by the Gestapo. They recognized him from the ghetto and they suspected he had a hand in helping some Jews escape. He was sent to Auschwitz, the horrible death camp, where he was beaten by the Germans. He never revealed the hiding place in his family's house.

As the Soviet army advanced towards Warsaw, the Germans began to retreat. However, before they left, they started to shoot people at random. This reign of terror forced most of the population to flee the city. The Kozminskis hid with their Jewish friends in the shelter until the Soviets finally liberated Warsaw. They never abandoned the Jews in their care.

For their extraordinary heroism in saving so many Jewish lives, the entire Kozminski family is honored at Yad Vashem as "Righteous Among the Nations."

CHAPTER 11

Nicholas Winton

Nicholas Winton was a modest man. It wasn't until many years after World War II ended that his wife discovered his bravery. This Englishman saved hundreds of Czechoslovakian children from the Nazis.

When Winton was thirty, he was working as a clerk in a London office. England and Germany were not yet at war, but the mighty German army seemed ready to strike Czechoslovakia. People there were fleeing their homes, afraid of what might happen to them.

A friend asked if Winton could help out in a refugee camp run by the British government in Prague ("Prog"), the capital of Czechoslovakia. Most of the people in the camp were Jews. He readily agreed.

Winton worked with a British team aiding the frightened refugees, but he saw no one helping the children. He knew they were in great danger and decided to get the children out of the country as quickly as possible. He set up a small relief office in the hotel where he was staying. He told the parents he wanted to get their children out of harm's way, and they all begged for his help.

Nicholas organized the Czech *kindertransport* ("children's transport") and went back to London to find families willing to accept these children in their homes. It was difficult to persuade the families. They had to pay for the children's transportation to England and then feed and clothe them indefinitely.

Nicholas worked feverishly to arrange the homes and the transportation. Time was not on his side, for it appeared that war would break out shortly between England and Germany. He struggled for nine months but he was able to round up eight trains and transport over six hundred Jewish children to their new parents in England. These poor children had to say goodbye to their mothers and fathers, who stayed behind in Czechoslovakia. Most never saw their real parents again. Those who stayed behind were sent to concentration camps.

England and Germany were now at war with one another. Nicholas could no longer bring any children into England, and the *kindertransport* stopped running.

None of the poor children left behind survived the war. Over fifteen thousand Jewish children in Czechoslovakia were killed, but Winton gave life and a new home to hundreds of others. The parents of these children died knowing that their sons and daughters would survive the Nazi terror and grow up in a new country with caring foster parents.

Nicholas's *kindertransport* children grew up in England never realizing who saved their lives. He never told anyone of his heroic achievements. Many years after the war ended, his wife, Greta, found lists of children and letters from grateful parents in his old briefcase. She confronted him and he finally told her what he did to save all of these Jewish children.

When his exploits became known throughout the country, many honors were bestowed upon Nicholas Winton. He was knighted by the Queen of England, and many of his "adopted" children finally found out the truth. The children he saved grew up to be outstanding British citizens. Some became doctors or lawyers, writers or journalists, teachers or diplomats. One even was a member of the British Parliament. Sir Nicholas Winton, the gentile savior of so many, was honored by the State of Israel as "Righteous Among the Nations."

PART 3

Germans Who Defied Orders

CHAPTER 12

Alfred Rosner

Alfred Rosner grew up in a little town near Frankfurt, Germany. He had been a sickly child, and because of his health problems, he was not drafted into the German army like other men his age. Before the war broke out, Rosner, a Christian, worked in a clothing factory owned by a Jew. The owner was very kind to his employees and everyone got along with one another. It was one big happy family. However, when the war broke out, the Germans took over all factories owned by Jews. The Germans needed experienced manpower to run the factories, so they kept the skilled Jewish workers. They made any Jewish owner just one of the laborers. Since Rosner was a non-Jewish German, he was appointed manager of the clothing factory. This was a very important factory. They made uniforms for the German army and navy.

The Jewish men and women who were employed in the factories were protected from being deported to concentration camps. Rosner's Jewish workers were temporarily spared this horrible fate. He always treated those who worked for him with great kindness, and he brought them special rations.

Rosner was very disturbed by the persecution of the Jews. He did not agree with the Nazi policies. He thought that the German Jews were German citizens like himself and should not be subject to this terrible treatment. He felt they were entitled to his protection. Whenever there was a roundup of other Jews, Rosner personally went to the railroad yard where they were being held and demanded that they be released. He claimed that he needed them for his factory and that these Jews were essential for the war effort. Since the army needed uniforms badly, no one questioned him. The Jews Rosner picked were spared from certain death.

One day at a roundup, he saw a young Jewish woman about to be transported to a concentration camp. She appeared to be very weak and sickly. Rosner demanded that she be removed from the train. He claimed she was one of his workers. He took the woman to his home, fed her, and cared for her until she was well enough to work at the factory.

Every time Rosner learned from trusted friends at the railroad yard that a roundup was scheduled, he warned as many Jews as he could find so they could hide. He also took some Jews into his own home. Many Jewish lives were saved by Rosner's brave deeds. He risked his own life in doing this.

When the Germans realized they were losing the war, they became desperate and rounded up more and more Jews, including the Jews from Rosner's factory. He did everything he could to persuade the Nazis to leave his workers alone. He protested to the authorities and even tried to block the Gestapo from entering the factory. The Nazis charged Rosner as an enemy of the state. He was arrested, imprisoned, and executed as a traitor. This good Christian lost his life trying to save Jews from certain death.

In September 1995, Alfred Rosner was honored by the State of Israel at Yad Vashem as "Righteous Among the Nations."

CHAPTER 13

Heinz Drossel

Heinz Drossel was a German army officer. Although many officers were members of the Nazi party, Drossel refused to join. He didn't share their racist policies or their politics.

Heinz was born in Berlin, the capital of Germany. When he grew up he studied law. Soon after he passed his law examination he was drafted into the German army.

Heinz was first sent to France, then the Soviet Union. Since he was an educated man, he was appointed as an officer, but his political views were not known to his superiors. He still was vehemently opposed to the Nazis and much preferred peaceful solutions to problems. He thought Germany was wrong to start the war, and he was particularly upset about the persecution of the Jews.

When men under his command captured a Soviet officer, Drossel's superior ordered him to execute the prisoner. Heinz took the Soviet outside, but instead of shooting him as ordered, he arranged for his escape. If his superiors ever found out that the Soviet wasn't executed, Drossel himself would have been shot.

One day while on leave in Berlin, Drossel noticed a young woman walking alone. When she saw this German officer, she became very frightened and tried to hide. She knew she shouldn't have been out, because there was a curfew for Jews in Berlin. She was looking for food. Drossel approached her and, instead of arresting her as a good German officer would have done, he took this young woman back to his apartment and gave her food and money so she could find a safe place to hide.

Drossel also saved the life of a famous German Jewish scientist, Dr. Ernest Fontheim. This scientist, his wife, and her elderly parents were hiding from the Nazis in a small town near Berlin. A friendly neighbor told Fontheim that the Gestapo was looking for him and questioning the townspeople about his whereabouts. It so happened that this was the same town where Heinz Drossel's parents lived. It was fate that Heinz was on leave and visiting his parents that

week. Fontheim knew that the Drossel family opposed the Nazis and was sympathetic towards Jews. He appealed to them for help. Heinz took the scientist and his family back to his own apartment in Berlin, where he knew they would be safe. No one would search a German army officer's home.

Heinz risked certain death for aiding Jews. He would have been executed immediately if he'd been caught doing it. The German officer was sent back to the Soviet Union. The war was not going well for the Germans there and they were on the defensive as the Soviet army advanced. Heinz felt that the war would be over shortly. He was ordered by his commanding officer to attack the Soviet troops. He refused the order, asking, "Why spill more blood when the war will soon be over?" He was immediately arrested and imprisoned for refusing to obey the order. He knew he would be executed. Fortunately, the Soviet army captured the base where he was held prisoner, and he was taken prisoner by the Soviets. He was held captive for over a year, then finally released and sent home. He was one of the lucky ones. The Soviets, bent on revenge, were executing their German captives. However, they learned that Drossel was imprisoned by the Germans for refusing to attack the Soviet army, so they knew he wasn't a Nazi.

When Heinz returned to Berlin, he looked for Marianne, the young Jewish woman he had saved several years before. He finally found her living among the ruins of Berlin, and he married her. They lived a full and happy life, and Heinz became a famous judge in Germany. He instilled in his children the same virtues that his parents taught him—kindness, compassion, and humanity.

The scientist Heinz saved from the Nazis, Dr. Ernest Fontheim, moved with his family to the United States, where he became a professor at the University of Michigan.

This brave German officer risked his life many times over to save Jews, and in May 2000 the State of Israel recognized Heinz Drossel as "Righteous Among the Nations."

"I'm really glad that this story had a happy ending," Donna said to Toby when they finished reading.

"Yes, and I'm happy to learn that there were some Germans who defied Hitler's policies against the Jews," replied Toby. "I wish there were more."

CHAPTER 14

Oskar Schindler

Toby recognized this name from a movie she saw called *Schindler's List*. Now she was anxious to read the story of this famous German who saved many Jewish lives.

Oskar Schindler was an unlikely hero. He was a German, grew up in a wealthy family in Austria, and was friendly with high-ranking Nazi officials. He enjoyed the good life, partying and gambling with his rich friends. He lived a very lavish lifestyle.

Poland had the largest Jewish population in Europe. One of the cities in Poland, Krakow, had a very large and active Jewish community. When the Germans invaded Poland, they persecuted all of the Jews who lived in that country. Jews were beaten, their property and businesses were taken from them, and all Jews were forced to live in ghettos. Schindler, seeing an opportunity to make money, moved to Krakow. He made friends with all of the high-ranking Nazi officers and German officials there. He wined them and dined them, gave them lavish gifts, and made sure they recognized and trusted him as a loyal German. The Germans rewarded Schindler with an opportunity to buy at a very low price a factory that they confiscated from its Jewish owner. Naturally, Schindler saw an opportunity to make a great deal of money and agreed to buy the business. He also decided to keep all of the skilled Jewish workers to help run the factory. He didn't do it out of love for Jews but because he could pay them hardly any money and he needed them to work his new business.

Schindler's factory was very important to the German war effort because it manufactured ammunition for the army. When the Germans began to remove Jews from the ghetto to transport them to concentration camps, Schindler saw another opportunity to make money. He found some Jews who still had some money and persuaded them to invest in his factory. In return, they would be able to work there and be spared deportation. He designated all of his workers as essential to the army and bribed Nazi officials to allow them to remain in Krakow. Schindler's factory was making so much money that he was able to feed and house his Jews. He knew that they were essential to his business, so he treated them kindly and never abused them. The lucky men and women who worked for him were sheltered from the Nazi brutality.

More and more Jewish families were rounded up by the Germans and loaded at the railroad station into cattle cars, awaiting deportation to concentration camps. At this point, a strange transformation took place in Schindler's character. He was appalled when he saw all of these innocent men, women, and children herded into railroad cars and sent to an almost certain death. His opinion of his Nazi friends quickly changed when he saw how brutal and inhumane they were. He knew he had to do something to protect his Jews from this terrible fate. He referred to his Jewish workers as "my children."

With the Soviet army quickly advancing towards Poland, the Germans hastened the roundup of Jews for deportation. Schindler made a list of all of his workers whom he deemed absolutely essential. He was still highly regarded as a loyal German, so with a little bribe money, he was able to keep the Jews on his list safe from deportation. He even used his influence to pull some Jews off the trains, saying he needed more manpower for the factory. His business continued to operate, but now his workers were turning out defective bullets for German guns.

When the war ended, Schindler, now married, decided with his wife to move to Argentina. He bought a small farm and brought some of his Jewish workers along with him to work the land. After a few years he tired of the farm and went back to Germany. He gave the farm to the Jews he had brought with him. After his lavish spending, he did not have much money left and died a poor man.

Through the courageous efforts of this brave German, Oskar Schindler saved over nine hundred Jews from certain death. Schindler's list of Jewish workers protected them and spared their lives. He was far from a perfect human being, but sometimes people whom you would least expect become heroes.

In 1967, Oskar Schindler was honored by the State of Israel as "Righteous Among the Nations." He is buried in Israel, and several of his "Jewish children" take care of his gravesite. In 1993, Oskar's wife, Emilie, who helped him during those terrible years in Poland, was also honored as "Righteous Among the Nations." She is buried alongside her husband.

CHAPTER 15

Elisabeth Abegg

As Toby read these amazing stories, she learned that a small minority of Germans were opposed to the Nazi policies against the Jews. Many of these brave people risked their lives and fought back. A great majority of them were imprisoned as traitors. Most of them ended up in concentration camps alongside the Jews whom they had sought to protect.

"I'm so glad we live in America!" Donna exclaimed to Toby. "We can disagree with something our government is doing or saying, but we won't go to jail. We are free to speak out."

"That's in our Bill of Rights," replied Toby. "We studied that in our history class, remember?" Now Toby learned about another German hero who risked her life to help Jews escape from the Nazi terror in Germany.

Elisabeth Abegg ("*Ah*-beg") grew up in Strasbourg, Germany. This was a very Christian town, and the majority of the townspeople believed in the equality of man and the dignity of human life. They felt that all life was a precious gift from God and therefore must be protected. These principles had a profound influence on Elisabeth, and she joined the Quakers, a religious sect that taught that man was put on earth to do good deeds. That became her mission in life.

Elisabeth taught history in a very fashionable school in Berlin, the capital of Germany. She always tried to impress upon her students her own beliefs in equality and tolerance. Many of her students were Jewish. When a Nazi was appointed headmaster of her school, she was extremely upset. She resigned her position and took a similar one in a smaller school. That's when the Nazis marked her as politically unreliable. She was questioned repeatedly about her beliefs, and the Gestapo watched her every move. Elisabeth decided to retire from teaching, for she could no longer talk to her students freely.

Elisabeth was very fond of many of her Jewish pupils. She maintained discreet contact with them. When her closest Jewish friend

was arrested and sent to a concentration camp, Abegg felt that she must do something to help, no matter the risk involved.

Elisabeth shared her small apartment with her mother and sister. She quickly turned her flat into a hiding place for Jews. Working with her Quaker friends, she sheltered Jews in her apartment or found temporary hiding places for them elsewhere. Food was in short supply in Germany and almost everything was rationed, but she skimped on her own food in order to feed those she hid. Her mother and sister also shared their food. Elisabeth even provided special Friday-evening Sabbath meals for them whenever she could. Most who came to her apartment for help were complete strangers, but no one was ever turned away. Abegg was able to get forged papers that helped many of the Jews escape Germany. All of this activity took place in her small apartment in Berlin, where all of her neighbors were pro-Nazi. She could have been turned in to the Gestapo by any one of them, at any time.

Elisabeth felt she was not doing enough, so she organized an underground that smuggled Jewish families to Switzerland. She sold all of her jewelry and used the money to bribe the border guards. She continued her humanitarian work, never thinking of the danger to herself and her family.

When the war ended, many of the Jews she helped remained in contact with Elisabeth. They petitioned the State of Israel to recognize this brave woman for her heroism. On her eighty-fifth birthday, Elisabeth Abegg, a German Quaker, was honored as "Righteous Among the Nations."

PART 4

Royalty and Brave Clergy

CHAPTER 16

Princess Andrew of Greece

Toby was fascinated by the next story she and Donna read. She knew that there were rich people, poor people, diplomats, farmers, priests, and nuns who were heroes and saved many Jewish lives. Now she read the story of a member of the English royal family: Princess Andrew, mother-in-law of Queen Elizabeth II.

In 1903, Prince Andrew of Greece took a wife, Alice. Andrew was related to the ruling house in Great Britain. Alice took the name Princess Andrew. In 1913, the Second Balkan War broke out, with Greece fighting Bulgaria. The princess worked close to the war zone as a nurse, caring for wounded Greek soldiers. She and her husband were staying at the home of their Jewish friend, Haim ("Hyim") Cohen. After the war, her friendship with Cohen continued. A member of the Greek Parliament, he was very influential in politics.

Princess Andrew had five children. One of her sons became Prince Philip of Great Britain. After World War I (1914-18), there was a revolution in Greece. The people wanted to overthrow the monarchy. Princess Andrew fled to France with her family. They were given protection by the French government and lived there for a while.

There were many Greek refugees in France, seeking safety. Princess Andrew founded a charity to help feed those refugees and became involved in humanitarian work. She wanted to devote her life to caring for the poor and less fortunate. Becoming deeply religious, she joined the Greek Orthodox Church and began wearing the habit of a nun. She and her husband separated.

Her daughters all married Greek royalty. Her son, Prince Philip, went to England to live with his uncle, Lord Louis Mountbatten, a close friend and advisor to the British royal family. Princess Andrew eventually returned to Greece and lived in a small apartment. She continued her work with the Greek Red Cross, running a soup kitchen to feed the poor and homeless.

In 1943, the Germans occupied Greece. Although her good

Jewish friend, Haim Cohen, had died several years before, his wife and children were desperately trying to escape from the Nazis. Princess Andrew offered to hide them in her small apartment. She fed and sheltered Cohen's wife and five children until the end of the war. She knew the risk she was taking but felt it was her duty to protect them. She also helped smuggle many Jews out of the country to Spain and Switzerland.

When the war ended, Princess Andrew took her vows and founded a nursing order of Greek Orthodox nuns. When her son Prince Philip married Queen Elizabeth, she attended the wedding wearing her simple nun's habit. Here a princess sat in a simple grey frock among all the other royalty with their beautiful dresses and jewels. Nevertheless, she was a true princess among the royals. She continued her charitable work, caring for the sick and needy until 1969. She died in Buckingham Palace, and according to her wishes, she was buried under a Greek Orthodox church on the Mount of Olives in Israel.

Princess Andrew of Greece was named "Righteous Among the Nations" for sheltering the Cohen family during the Nazi occupation of Greece. This brave royal turned nun risked her life to save her Jewish friends and help other Jews escape to safety.

CHAPTER 17

Mother Maria Skobtsova

Toby and Donna read about a nun who saved many Jews in France and was herself imprisoned by the Nazis. They were very touched by the story of this unusual woman named Elizabeth Skobtsova.

She was born in 1891 in a small village in Russia. When Elizabeth grew up, she became friends with many well-known Russian writers, poets, and political thinkers. Their philosophy helped shaped her own life and beliefs. Elizabeth was a very strong-minded woman. She was twice married and divorced. After her second divorce, she became very interested in religion and decided to attend a monastery to take religious training.

There was unrest among the Russian people at that time, and Elizabeth herself was unhappy with the ruling government. She joined a revolutionary party and became a radical. She had to flee Russia because of her political activities and spent several years traveling throughout Europe, eventually settling down in Paris, France. She lived in poverty for many years, making cheap jewelry that she sold to tourists. There were days when she had to eat at a soup kitchen. Many other Russian radicals fled their country and settled in Paris. Some were the same social activists Elizabeth knew back home, and she quickly joined them and formed the Russian student Christian movement. She was equally comfortable discussing politics and religion with her friends. She became so involved in religion that she decided to become a nun in the Russian Orthodox Church, taking the name Maria.

When the Germans occupied Paris in 1940, Mother Maria opened a soup kitchen and fed the poor and sick who came to her daily. She turned no one away. Maria was very aware of the brutal Nazi persecution of the Jews and felt it was her responsibility to help them in any way she could. She preached to all who would listen that the battle against the Jews was also a battle against Christianity. She urged all true Christians to wear the yellow Star of David that the Nazis forced

the Jews to wear. She and her good friend Friar Dimitri Klepenen forged baptismal certificates, which she passed out to Jews. This gave them new identities and helped many Jewish families avoid the Nazi terror. She also took a great risk and hid several Jews in her house.

One terrible day in 1942, thousands of French Jews were rounded up by the Nazis for deportation to concentration camps. They were being held in a large housing complex in a Paris suburb waiting for transport. With the help of several trusted friends, Mother Maria managed to smuggle hundreds of Jewish children out of the complex by hiding them in large garbage bins. She gave them forged baptismal certificates and they were able to blend in with the general population. Despite the danger, she went again and again to the complex to smuggle food in and smuggle children out.

The Nazis became aware of her activities and warned her several times, but Maria was defiant and continued to help the Jews. She joined a small Jewish resistance movement that was active in hiding Jews and smuggling them out of the country. It was inevitable that she would be caught. She was sent to Ravensbruck ("*Rav*-inz-brook") concentration camp. At Ravensbruck she worked at hard labor alongside all the other prisoners. Many were sick and starving, and this good nun soon became sick herself. Even though she was weak from hunger and disease, she continued to comfort and minister to everyone in the camp. On March 31, 1945, with the Soviet army close to liberating Ravensbruck, Mother Maria Skobtsova died.

The Russian Orthodox Church recognized this nun's heroism and she became Saint Maria. People from all faiths were present in the church when she was honored. Many of them were Jews she saved from going to the death camps. For her bravery and sacrifice in saving so many Jewish lives, Elizabeth Skobtsova, known as Mother Maria, was proclaimed by the State of Israel as "Righteous Among the Nations."

CHAPTER 18

Pastor Andre Trocme

The small village of Le Chambon in southeastern France and its Protestant pastor, Andre Trocme, saved over five thousand Jewish lives. The people of this village were peace-loving farmers. They strongly opposed the Nazi persecution of the Jews and hated even more the French officials who collaborated with the Nazis. Many of those government officials were violently anti-Semitic and openly friendly towards the Germans.

Pastor Trocme was taught at an early age to love and care for all mankind regardless of religion. He vowed to devote his life to help those in need. Trocme's message to his parishioners was that human life was precious and everyone had to do whatever was necessary to protect it. His congregation embraced his teachings, and he became the spiritual leader of this humble village.

When France was occupied by the Germans in 1940, the country was divided in to two parts. The Germans occupied the northern part, and the southern part was governed by French officials who were pro-German. This southern part of France would then be referred to as Vichy ("Vee-shee"). The French officials there did whatever the German authorities told them to do and did nothing to prevent the persecution of Jews living in their territory. The Nazis told them to round up all the Jews and get them ready for deportation to concentration camps. When Trocme saw this decree posted in his village, he gave a sermon in his church urging the villagers to resist this order. He said this vile decree was contrary to God's teachings. His was a simple call of duty for all Christians to help the Jews in their time of need. The good people of Le Chambon heeded his call. They saw their Jewish neighbors in danger and they were prepared to help them.

Everyone was asked to hide and protect a Jewish family. The Jews were given refuge in private homes, on farms, and even in public buildings. They were provided with food and shelter for as long as they wanted. They were given forged identifications cards and many worked on the farms as laborers.

When the Nazis asked the villagers who these people were who were living with them and working on their farms, the villagers simply called them relatives. If the Jews were asked to produce their identification papers, they had the forged papers ready to show the Germans. Not a single Jew was turned over to the Nazis. The villagers put themselves at great risk by doing this, for they knew they could be imprisoned themselves.

The Jewish children were especially important to the villagers and they took great care to see that they were protected. They went to school with the other children and were treated like they belonged to the village. Many Jews used Le Chambon as a place to hide before being smuggled into Switzerland, which was a neutral country and not at war. Some of the small villages surrounding Le Chambon followed its example and also hid many Jewish refugees.

These great acts of courage put the lives of all the villagers at risk. When Nazi officials asked if there were any Jews in the village, the people of course denied that there were any living there. The Germans and their Vichy French officials didn't believe them and said they knew that they were hiding Jews. Pastor Trocme boldly told them that anyone who comes to his village seeking help would be protected. He wouldn't ask their religion nor would he care. He only saw these poor people as children of God who needed help. This act of defiance infuriated the Germans, and they said they were sending buses to the village to round up the Jews. Again the pastor told them that there were no Jews in the village, and even if there were, he would not hand them over. This infuriated the Nazis even more, and they demanded a list of everyone who lived in Le Chambon. Trocme said he would not hand over such a list. The Nazis searched all of the houses in the little village but did not find a single Jew. They were all hidden under the church. The buses left empty.

Time and again the Nazis came to Le Chambon looking for Jews. The people were always warned ahead of time that the buses were coming, and all the Jews again were hidden under the church or in the surrounding countryside. When the buses would leave, the villagers would take the Jews home.

This game of hide and seek couldn't last forever. On the Nazis' suspicions alone, Andre Trocme was arrested and imprisoned. He was repeatedly beaten and questioned but wouldn't reveal the secret of Le Chambon. When the Nazis eventually released him, he had to go into hiding. He knew they were watching his every move and would arrest him again and this time probably shoot him. Still, the villagers continued to hide and protect their "Old Testament brothers," as they called the Jews. Unfortunately, when the Nazis raided the village again, they found some frightened Jewish children who were hiding. They were rounded up and sent to concentration camps. Most of them died there.

The village of Le Chambon saved over five thousand Jewish lives by resisting the Nazis and their Vichy friends. This was a remarkable feat by these humble French farmers and their heroic pastor. In 1990, the State of Israel planted two trees at Yad Vashem. One was for the French village of Le Chambon and the other for Pastor Andre Trocme and his wife, Magda, all honored as "Righteous Among the Nations." Many books were written and movies made to commemorate the heroics of these Righteous Gentiles.

CHAPTER 19

Father Jacques

It is unfortunate that not everyone helped rescue Jews in the countries the Germans occupied during World War II. Many didn't care; many were anti-Semitic and happy that the Jews were being persecuted; and many were afraid of getting caught and being sent to concentration camps along with the Jews.

However, many priests, nuns, and pastors hid thousands of Jewish children in their monasteries, churches, and schools. Many of these children were placed with kind families who felt it was their moral obligation to save Jews from imprisonment and probable death. These families were aware of the dangers they faced, but these ordinary people did extraordinary things. Some of these brave people were poor farmers, shopkeepers, bakers, or butchers. Some were doctors or teachers or even police officers. There were rich people and poor people. These rescuers lived in many different countries, and they viewed Jews and other victims of Nazi oppression as fellow human beings. These people all had one thing in common. They knew that everyone was a child of God and that all life was precious. Father Jacques ("Jock") was that kind of person.

He was born and grew up in France. He became a Carmelite friar and head of a school run by the Carmelites. Father Jacques de Jesus was very angry at the Nazi policies against the Jews. He knew that being sent to concentration camps meant certain death. Many young Jewish boys were sent to camps where they were forced to work at hard labor for the Germans, building roads and repairing bridges and railroad lines that had been bombed by the American Air Force. They were given meager rations to live on and worked from early morning to late evening. Many died from malnutrition and disease. When they were too weak to work anymore, they were shot.

Father Jacques hid several Jewish boys in his school. He enrolled them as students under false names. The Gestapo found out about his illegal activities and arrested him, along with his Jewish students.

They were sent to Auschwitz, the horrible concentration camp, where most of them eventually died.

Father Jacques was beaten by the Germans for helping the Jews. He was forced to work at hard labor. The good friar never lost his spirit or his faith in God. He shared his food with the other starving prisoners and even held secret Christian services for all who wanted to participate. In May 1945, the American army finally liberated the camp and rescued him along with all of the other prisoners. Father Jacques was so weak from malnutrition that he contracted tuberculosis. He died several months after being rescued.

Because of his heroism, the State of Israel honored his memory at Yad Vashem. In 1985, Father Jacques de Jesus was declared "Righteous Among the Nations." A movie about this hero was made by a famous French filmmaker and dedicated to the memory of this good priest. Called *Au Revoir Les Enfants* (*Goodbye, Children*), it won many awards. The United States Holocaust Memorial Museum also has an exhibit honoring this Righteous Gentile.

CHAPTER 20

Father Pierre Marie Benoit

Father Benoit ("Ben-*wah*") was a French national living in a monastery in Rome. When war broke out between France and Italy, he moved into a monastery in Marseilles ("Mar-*say*"), France.

Marseilles was in the southern part of France, now governed by the Vichy French. They were sympathetic to the Germans. When the Nazis who occupied the northern part of the country enacted laws against Jews throughout France, Vichy France was only too happy to carry them out. Many frightened Jews tried to flee southern France for neutral nations such as Spain and Switzerland. They felt they would be safe there. Father Benoit pledged to himself to help these fleeing Jews any way he could. Using his connections with Protestant and Greek Orthodox organizations, he was able to obtain forged papers and find temporary hiding places for Jews. He helped smuggle many of them across the border. Soon word of his assistance spread among the Jews, and his monastery was overflowing with people begging for his help. The little printing press in the basement worked overtime, churning out thousands of false baptismal certificates for Jews who had to pretend to be Christian.

The Spanish and Swiss governments became very concerned about all these refugees flooding their countries. Many had no money and nowhere to live. They were only able to carry a few possessions with them when they crossed the border. These two countries wanted to close off their borders. Father Benoit met with the Italian commissioner in France (Germany and Italy were friends and allies at the time) and persuaded him to refrain from taking any further action against the Jews. He also met secretly with Pope Pius XII and presented a plan to transfer the Jews through Italy to North Africa. However, the Gestapo discovered these plans and Father Benoit had to flee France and become a refugee himself. He moved back to Rome and continued his compassionate work on behalf of the Jews. He persisted in supplying false documents for Jews that allowed them to live under assumed Christian names. He

also obtained scarce ration cards for food, pretending they were for non-Jewish refugees.

Father Benoit placed himself at great personal risk, but he had a profound commitment to humanitarian values and the preservation of the rights of all people to live in freedom, regardless of religion.

When Rome was liberated from Nazi rule in 1944, many in the Jewish community, living under assumed Christian names, praised this humble monk as their savior. Hundreds of Jews owe their lives to this Righteous Gentile who risked his own life to save them. On April 26, 1966, the State of Israel recognized this French priest's heroism and bestowed upon him the honor of "Righteous Among the Nations."

CHAPTER 21

Rev. Waitstill and Martha Sharp

This is the story of two ordinary people who did extraordinary deeds to save hundreds of Jewish lives. Waitstill Sharp, a Unitarian minister from Wellesley, Massachusetts, and his wife, Martha, put aside their concerns for their personal safety and went to Prague, Czechoslovakia, at a time when hundreds of refugees were streaming into that city from countries occupied by the Germans. Both Waitstill and Martha were highly educated. They had deep religious convictions and they knew the dangers of their mission in Prague. However, they felt that it was their duty to go and help, no matter the risks involved. A month later, Czechoslovakia itself was invaded. The Sharps then helped secure food, shelter, medicine, and—most important—visas allowing Jews and non-Jews to escape from the Nazis.

The Germans were very suspicious of these Americans and watched them closely. Waitstill and Martha decided to go to France, which was not yet occupied by the Germans. France was a relatively safe haven for many prominent Jewish scientists, writers, and teachers who had left their own countries. But when the Germans occupied France, these Jewish refugees were in great danger. The reverend and his wife organized the Unitarian Service Committee, which raised money to help these people. They used these funds to bribe the border guards so many of these Jews could escape to safe countries. Another American, Varian Fry, helped the Sharps in this effort to rescue Jews.

Martha often worked apart from her husband. They would sometimes be in different sections of the country. She saw firsthand the conditions of the refugee camps and brought milk to the undernourished children. Working with her husband, she was able to forge visas and identification cards for these children and smuggle them out of the country.

Many of the adults they saved settled in the United States or Israel. One of them was Otto Meyerhof, who had won the Nobel

prize for medicine in 1922. This brave couple also saved writers, composers, doctors, and scientists who in turn were able to serve mankind.

The Sharps returned to the United States to travel and raise money for various relief organizations for European refugees. They also spread the word about the horrible persecution of the Jews by the Nazis. Theirs was a lonely voice because not many paid attention to their horror stories. Frustrated by this apparent lack of interest, the Sharps returned to Europe after the war. When the American army liberated many of these death camps, the truth of what the Sharps had been preaching all along was finally confirmed to the world. With the backing of their Unitarian Service Committee, they helped Jews who survived the concentration camps relocate to other countries.

Martha and Waitstill divorced and went their separate ways. He began preaching again and became a civil rights activist. He never talked much about his wartime activities. He died in 1984. Martha became involved in politics. She ran for Congress and lost after a smear campaign that painted her as a radical. She moved to Washington, D.C., married a Jewish businessman, and worked for the Truman administration. She became involved in numerous civic and charitable organizations and tried to keep in touch with some of the children she saved. She died in 1999 at the age of ninety-four.

Even though the Sharps divorced, what they did they did together, hand in hand. Therefore, it was appropriate that the State of Israel honored them together as "Righteous Among the Nations." Only one other American has been so honored. The Unitarian Church and the United States Holocaust Memorial Museum also recognized their heroism. They saved the lives of hundreds of Jewish and non-Jewish men, women, and children who grew up to be productive citizens and never forgot their "guardian angels," Rev. Waitstill and Martha Sharp.

PART 5

Heroic Diplomats

CHAPTER 22

Varian Fry

One of the few Americans to be honored at Yad Vashem is Varian Fry. He was a Harvard-educated newspaper editor from New York City. He helped save thousands of refugees who escaped from the Nazis and fled to France. Among them were such prominent Jews as painters Marc Chagall and Max Ernst, sculptor Jacques Lipchitz, and writer Hannah Arendt. Some of Europe's greatest artists and writers were brought to the United States thanks to his emergency rescue committee.

Fry visited Germany in 1935 and witnessed firsthand the brutal persecution of Jews in that country. He knew something must be done to help these poor victims, but unfortunately, his was a lonely voice. Varian raised $3,000 in the United States as an emergency fund and left for France to see if he could help the refugees there. This was a pretty good sum of money in those days. He planned to use these funds to obtain passports for several Jewish refugees so he could bring them to the United States.

Varian then had to convince the U.S. government that admitting these refugees was the humanitarian thing to do. Many people in this country were suspicious of "foreigners" at that time and were afraid that these people would take jobs away from Americans. During the 1930s, America was going through a depression and jobs were scarce. Some also thought these newcomers might actually be spies. Varian enlisted the help of Eleanor Roosevelt, the wife of the president. She aided him in his cause and was able to convince several government officials to allow the refugees to enter the country.

Fry returned to France again. He tried to convince the French authorities to give these Jewish refugees exit visas. Many in the French government were sympathetic towards Germany and were suspicious of Fry's activities. He was watched closely and could have been deported back to the United States at any time. Varian also pleaded with the Spanish and Portuguese embassies to issue visas and allow some of these Jewish refugees into their countries. He met with very limited success, but despite the danger, he continued his work. Most of the refugees were Jews, but Varian Fry offered aid to almost anyone who asked.

When hundreds of people lined up outside his hotel in France, Fry realized he couldn't do this all by himself. He quickly found some young Americans and Europeans who were eager to work with him. Together they created several escape routes over the mountains to Spain. They forged passports that the refugees used to book passage on ships sailing from France.

In addition to planning these escapes, Fry spoke out against many of the camps in France that held these refugees. When Germany invaded France in May 1940, these German refugees were considered enemy aliens. Many of them died in the camps from hunger and disease. Throughout the following year, Fry managed to smuggle hundreds of Jews out of France. He knew he was monitored very closely by the authorities.

Fry was finally arrested and expelled from France as an enemy of the state. He returned to the United States. Even though America was not yet at war with Germany, U.S. officials also disapproved of his work and refused to renew his passport for future foreign travels. So he toured the United States speaking out against the Vichy French government, which he claimed was just as bad as the Nazis. He was one of the first to warn about the Holocaust. Not many people listened to him, including his own government. He was considered a wild radical.

As we now know, his concerns were correct. After the war, Fry was finally recognized for his heroism and awarded the French Medal of Honor. He moved to Connecticut to live a quiet life and teach. He died in obscurity. Twenty-four years after his death, he was recognized by Israel as "Righteous Among the Nations," one of only three Americans to receive this high honor.

CHAPTER 23

Raoul Wallenberg

Toby was anxious to read about this Righteous Gentile. She already knew that he was one of the most revered heroes in Israel for his role in saving the lives of so many Jews during the war. If Judaism had saints, he would be one of them.

Raoul Wallenberg was born into one of the most famous and wealthy families in Sweden. His father was a high-ranking officer in the Swedish army, and his relatives were famous bankers. It was assumed that Raoul would also go into banking, but he was more interested in studying architecture. A brilliant student, he learned to speak several languages in school and became fluent in Russian. Like all young men his age, Raoul was drafted into the Swedish army. After he completed his military service, he traveled to the United States to study architecture at the University of Michigan. He graduated with top honors and returned to Sweden to pursue his career. His father sent him to South Africa to work for a Swedish company. After a few years, he grew impatient and left for Haifa ("*Hi*-fah") in Palestine (now the State of Israel). While working there for a Dutch bank, he met many Jews who fled Germany because of their persecution by Hitler. They told him horror stories of the Nazi brutality, and these tales affected him deeply. Wallenberg was a very sensitive and humane individual. Although he wasn't Jewish, he traced his family tree and discovered that one of his ancestors who came to Sweden in the 1700s was Jewish.

Raoul made friends easily and knew many important people in the business world. He met a Hungarian Jew who was the director of a Swedish food business, and he became a partner in the business. As he traveled throughout Europe to promote his business, he witnessed firsthand the persecution of the Jews, particularly in France, which at that time was occupied by Germany. Sweden was a neutral country, and that allowed him to travel all over Europe. He also visited Hungary, where his business partner lived. Over 700,000 Jews were living in Hungary. While there, Wallenberg became aware of Hitler's plan to exterminate the Jews in Europe.

Hungary had been allied with Germany against the Soviets. But the Germans were losing, and Hitler felt that the Hungarians were not very reliable, so he invaded and occupied that country. Then the persecution of the Jews living there began. The Germans started rounding them up and deporting them to concentration camps. In desperation, many Jews sought help from countries that were not at war with Germany. If those countries issued them visas and allowed them to enter, they might be safe. The Germans had to honor those visas.

By the time Wallenberg was in Budapest, the capital of Hungary, many Hungarian Jewish families had already been deported to concentration camps. Raoul appealed to the king of Sweden to persuade the German-controlled Hungarian government to stop these deportations. Since the king knew the powerful Wallenberg family, he sent a strong letter of protest to the Hungarians, and the deportations were temporarily suspended.

The king appointed Wallenberg as an official of the Swedish embassy in Hungary. He headed a department that was responsible for aiding Jews. He devised a clever plan to protect Jewish families from the Nazis. He rented several buildings in Budapest and erected signs proclaiming that they belonged to the Swedish embassy. Since Sweden was a neutral country, the Germans could not enter those buildings. Wallenberg persuaded several other neutral countries to follow his example and rent buildings to shelter Jews.

Raoul also printed up fake passports from the Swedish embassy. They had all the right signatures and stamps on them, along with the Swedish crown. He gave these to the Jews in his buildings.

The Soviet army was advancing towards Hungary and would soon invade. There was an organization in Hungary known as the "Arrow Cross." This organization was working with the Germans and also hated the Jews. The Nazis felt that that the German-controlled Hungarian government was being too lenient towards the Jews, so they installed the leader of the Arrow Cross as head of the government. This was very bad news for the Jews, because the Arrow Cross wanted to resume the deportations. Raoul knew he had to do something quickly.

He rented thirty more houses and put the Swedish flag on them. Over 15,000 Hungarian Jews were sheltered and protected in those buildings.

Raoul printed more fake passports to give to the Jews, but the deportations soon resumed. At one point, the Germans and their Hungarian friends rounded up a large number of Jewish men, women, and children and forced them to march 200 miles to a concentration camp in Austria. It was bitterly cold and snowing. The Jews had no warm clothing and were given no food along the march. Even the German soldiers who guarded them complained to their superiors about this inhumane treatment. The guards saw old men, women, and children who were sickly and starving drop by the wayside. They were either shot or left to die. Wallenberg marched alongside the group, handing out food and medicine wherever he could. He tried to save as many as he could.

Many Jews were transported to concentration camps on cattle

cars. Wallenberg ran alongside these trains as they were about to leave, throwing his fake passports inside the cars in hopes that the Germans would honor them. Then he would stand in the middle of the tracks in front of the train, demanding on behalf of the Swedish government that the Jews who had his passports be allowed to leave. Many of the guards were so intimidated that they did allow some of the Jews off the trains, but unfortunately not enough of them.

The Jews in Budapest were forced to live in a ghetto. Conditions were horrible, and many were dying from starvation or disease. Wallenberg made friends with a high-ranking officer in the Arrow Cross who showed some sympathy towards the Jews. He learned from him that the Germans were planning to execute all the remaining Jews in the ghetto. Wallenberg demanded that his friend put a stop to these executions.

This officer was no dummy. He realized that Germany was losing the war and the Soviets were approaching the border. He felt that it would be in his own best interests if he obeyed Wallenberg's demands, so he stopped the planned execution of 97,000 Jews who remained in the ghetto. This Swedish diplomat put himself at great risk to save as many Jewish lives as possible.

The Soviet army finally invaded Hungary, forcing the Germans to retreat. Over 120,000 Jews in that country were liberated from the Nazi terror. Wallenberg greeted the Soviets as friends and told them he represented the Swedish government. He mentioned to them the Jews he sheltered in his safe houses. They couldn't understand why this Swedish diplomat risked his life to save Jews. They were suspicious of his motives. Perhaps he was a German spy.

The Soviets arrested Raoul Wallenberg and sent him to Moscow for questioning. The Swedish government had been expecting him to return home when Hungary was liberated. When they didn't hear from Wallenberg for several weeks, they questioned the Soviets about his disappearance. The Soviets made up several different stories. First they told Sweden he had died of a heart attack in prison. Then they changed the story and said he was killed by the Germans as he was leaving to greet the Soviet army.

Some German prisoners said upon their release from a Soviet prison that they saw Wallenberg and that the Soviets executed him for fear he was a spy. To this day, no one knows what actually happened to this heroic diplomat. Most think he was killed by the

Soviets. The real story may never be known. The Swedish government was not aggressive about tracking him down. Many other governments were curious about his disappearance but made no attempt to find him. What an unfortunate ending for such a great man.

When the story finally became known of what Raoul Wallenberg did in Hungary to save so many Jewish lives, he was recognized by many countries around the world. Streets and plazas in Israel bear his name, and in 1963 Raoul Wallenberg was recognized as "Righteous Among the Nations." In 1981, the United States made him an honorary citizen. Canada did the same in 1985 and the State of Israel in 1986.

CHAPTER 24

Per Anger

Per Anger was a Swedish diplomat who worked closely with Raoul Wallenberg in Hungary. He was responsible for saving thousands of Hungarian Jews from the concentration camps.

Anger had an interesting career. He was born in Sweden and studied law. Soon after graduating from law school, like all young men he was drafted into the Swedish army. When he completed his military service, he was offered a diplomatic post with the Swedish embassy in Berlin. He witnessed firsthand Hitler's persecution of the Jews in Germany. Extremely upset, he sent notes to his government about this treatment.

After working in Germany for a short time, he was sent back to Sweden, where he worked on Swedish-Hungarian trade relations. He worked very well with the Hungarians and was appointed second in charge of the Swedish embassy in Hungary. When the Germans occupied that country, the situation for the Jews worsened. They were openly persecuted and forced to wear yellow stars on their clothing. Soon the deportations of Jews to concentration camps began. At this point, the entire Swedish embassy was mobilized to save the Jews.

Jews who had relatives or even friends in Sweden flocked to the embassy seeking help. Anger came up with the idea of issuing travel documents to these people in place of real passports. A travel document was always issued when a Swedish citizen traveling outside of Sweden lost his or her passport. It served as a substitute passport. Anger persuaded the German-controlled Hungarian government to recognize the people who held these documents as Swedish citizens.

The Germans and their Hungarian allies had no choice but to accept these "passports" from a neutral country. Word spread among Jews in other countries, and soon thousands streamed into Hungary, seeking help from the Swedish embassy. More personnel were needed to process all of these requests, and Raoul Wallenberg was sent to help Anger.

Wallenberg came up with the idea of making these travel documents look like real passports. He put the Swedish crown on them and even had them printed with the Swedish colors. It was a masterpiece of forgery that fooled the Germans and Hungarians.

Both Anger and Wallenberg went to the railroad yards where the Jews were herded into cattle cars, awaiting deportation. They passed out as many of the forged passports as they had and angrily demanded that their "Jewish Swedish" citizens be released. Some were and many were not. Time and time again they appeared at the stations whenever there was a roundup, saving as many Jews as they could with their fake passports. The Germans caught on to their little game and began to watch them closely. They could have been imprisoned at any time.

Bombs were falling as the Soviets approached Budapest, and the Swedish government was afraid for the safety of the embassy employees. Instead of heeding their government's advice to come home, Anger and the rest of the Swedes chose to stay and help whomever they could. They spent many of their days in underground shelters. When the Soviets liberated Hungary, they put all of the Swedish personnel in what they called protective custody. Anger was questioned about his role in the war and particularly about his fake passports. Wallenberg was taken to Moscow and never heard from again. Per returned to Sweden and began searching for his friend. He spread information throughout the world about Wallenberg's heroic deeds and asked the heads of several governments to investigate his disappearance. Some did but without any results, and many quietly dropped the search.

Per Anger continued his diplomatic career as Sweden's ambassador to Australia and then to Canada. He received many awards because of his heroic efforts in Hungary. In 1982, the State of Israel named him "Righteous Among the Nations" and planted a tree for him next to one for his friend Raoul Wallenberg. Together they put their own lives in danger and rescued thousands of Jews during World War II. This Righteous Gentile died in 2002.

CHAPTER 25

Carl Lutz

Few people are aware of this Swiss diplomat who saved the lives of 60,000 Hungarian Jews from the concentration camps. Even his own government didn't acknowledge his heroism until many years after the war ended.

Switzerland was one of the few neutral countries during World War II. They didn't favor any side in this terrible war, so they were not occupied by the Germans. Carl Lutz was assigned to the Swiss embassy in Budapest, Hungary as vice-consul. Before the war, Lutz worked in Palestine (now the State of Israel). Carl became friends with many Germans who also worked in Palestine, and they considered him a real ally. This worked in his favor when he was sent to Hungary.

Lutz was raised as a strict Methodist. He went to church every Sunday and even taught Sunday school. He was a God-fearing man, and when he saw what the Nazis and their Hungarian allies were doing to the Jews, he knew he had to help them. Carl decided to issue safe-conduct passes to Switzerland to as many Jews as possible. This would allow them to then go to Palestine, where many Jews lived. They would be out of harm's way. The passes issued by the Swiss embassy meant that the Jews were protected by a neutral country. The Germans honored these passes because of their friendship with and respect for Carl Lutz. They had no desire to offend the Swiss government.

Like Wallenberg, Lutz rented many buildings in Budapest and declared them Swiss property. Jews were sheltered in these buildings, and the Germans could not enter the Swiss property and attempt to seize the Jews living there. This Swiss diplomat continued to issue safe-conduct passes to entire families, counting them as one unit. He was only allowed by his government to issue one pass to one person. Counting families as one unit enabled Lutz to issue more passes and help entire families to escape the Nazis, but it also violated Swiss orders. The Swiss warned him several times to stop or

he would be sent home. He ignored these warnings and continued his work saving Jews.

Now even Carl's German friends were becoming suspicious of his activities. They were watching his every move. Lutz knew he was taking a big risk but continued to issue passes. This simple piece of paper bearing his signature saved the lives of tens of thousands of Jews. The Swiss government finally accused Carl Lutz of overstepping his authority and he was ordered home. When the war ended, he was demoted and given a minor job in the Swiss diplomatic corps. This effectively ended his promising career. He was never promoted and was virtually ignored by the Swiss. After several decades, he became depressed and suffered a nervous breakdown. He died shortly thereafter, virtually unknown except by the thousands of Jews whose lives he saved in Hungary.

In 1995, twenty years after his death, the Swiss government finally recognized this hero. This Righteous Gentile was honored with a stamp issued by Switzerland. However, Israel recognized Lutz even before his own government did and named a street after him in Haifa. In 1964, Carl Lutz was named "Righteous Among the Nations" and formally took his rightful place among the heroes at Yad Vashem.

CHAPTER 26

Senpo Sugihara

"Oh, here is the Japanese name I read outside," Toby proclaimed to Donna. "His country was actually fighting with Germany against us."

"He must really be a hero if he defied the Nazis," Donna replied. They began to read this man's story.

In July 1940, a large crowd of frightened Polish Jews surrounded the Japanese consulate (part of an embassy) in Kovno, Lithuania. They had escaped from Poland. They knew what was happening to the Jews in Germany, and when Poland was invaded, they were afraid of the same fate. In Kovno, they had appealed to the Dutch consulate to allow them to escape to Curaçao ("Kyur-uh-*sow*"), a Dutch island near Venezuela. They were told they must travel to Japan to reach Curaçao, so a Japanese transit visa was required.

Senpo Sugihara was an official at the Japanese consulate in Kovno. He sent a message to his superiors requesting permission to issue these visas to the Jewish refugees who were flooding the consulate. This request was promptly denied. Japan did not want foreigners passing through their country, and they also did not want to offend Germany, their friend and close ally. Sugihara was angered by this rejection from his government. Unlike most of the Japanese, he was a devout Christian and belonged to the Russian Orthodox Church. His wife, also a Christian, urged him to help these Jews escape. He risked losing his job, but he went to the Soviet consulate in Kovno to seek their assistance. In order to get to Japan, it was necessary to go through the Soviet Union, and therefore the Jews first needed a transit visa from the Soviet Union. After listening to Sugihara's impassioned plea, the Soviets agreed to issue the visas. Once the Jews had the Soviet visas, Senpo had to issue his Japanese visas. He was torn between duty and humanity. He knew that if he issued the visas, Japan would be furious. He could lose his job and be sent home. He issued the visas anyway.

When Japan realized what he was doing, Sugihara was ordered home immediately. He ignored their order and continued to issue visas to the Jews who were fortunate enough to have their Soviet papers. Japan then ordered him to report to their embassy in Berlin, where the Germans could watch him closely. Sugihara had no choice but to obey. Even at the railroad station, while waiting for the train to take him to Germany, he continued to issue visas as quickly as he could. As the train pulled out of the station, he tearfully begged forgiveness from those who were not able to get one of his visas. That's the kind of person Senpo Sugihara was.

After a short time at his embassy in Berlin, he was sent to many different Japanese embassies in Europe. In 1941, Japan bombed Pearl Harbor, drawing the United States into the war. After many years of brutal fighting, Germany finally surrendered in May 1945. Japan kept fighting on, even though they were losing the war. The Soviet Union declared war on Japan, and in August 1945, the United States dropped the atomic bomb on Hiroshima and Nagasaki. Japan surrendered in September, and World War II was officially over.

Sugihara and his family were imprisoned by the Soviets and released after two years. When they returned to Japan, they found out Sugihara was fired from the diplomatic service for disobeying orders. He was a broken man, and it was difficult for him to find work. He did odd jobs, even working at an army PX, which is a large store for military families. He left that job and worked for a Soviet company until he retired a poor and sick man.

Senpo often wondered what happened to the many Jews he saved from the Nazis. He didn't regret for a moment what he did. Many of those Jews spread the word of how they were saved by this gentle man. They never forgot that they owed their lives to his bravery.

The Sugihara family was invited to Israel, where they received many awards from both the Israeli and the United States governments. Senpo's visas saved 4,000 Jewish lives. Many Jews who escaped through Japan stayed in that country and formed a large Jewish community. Some went to Palestine and helped form the new Jewish State of Israel. Others went to the United States and became doctors, lawyers, teachers, and businessmen.

For his acts of kindness and bravery, Senpo Sugihara was honored as "Righteous Among the Nations," and in 1985 he and his wife were granted full Israeli citizenship. Several streets in Lithuania are named Sugihara Street, and finally, after many long years, the

Japanese government recognized his heroic deeds. A statue in Tokyo has been erected in his honor.

Now Toby knew why a tree was planted for a Japanese man at Yad Vashem.

CHAPTER 27

Aristides de Sousa Mendes

Probably half a million Jewish lives were saved by foreign diplomats who defied their own governments' orders and issued visas allowing them to escape to neutral countries. Toby read about Wallenberg, Anger, Lutz, and Sugihara. Now she read about another brave diplomat, Aristides Mendes of Portugal.

Mendes was born into an aristocratic Portuguese family, studied law, and entered the diplomatic service of his country. After several postings to various countries, he was appointed head consul in Bordeaux ("Bor-*doh*"), in the south of France, which was controlled by the Vichy government. This government was certainly no friend to the Jews. Jewish refugees from northern France arrived in the south, praying for a precious visa that would enable them to continue through neutral Spain and Portugal and finally to countries outside of Europe. This was a long and dangerous journey, but it was the only hope these poor Jews had to escape from the Germans.

However, the leaders of Spain and Portugal were pretty friendly with the Germans and not anxious to help or shelter Jews. These countries wanted to avoid being invaded as France had been. They closed their borders to the fleeing refugees unless they had proper travel visas. Furthermore, the Portuguese government refused to issue visas to refugees.

Mendes was determined to help these Jews and defied his country's ban on issuing visas. Using his authority, he issued transit visas for entry into Portugal. These ensured passage through Spain as well, as long as the visa holders did not stay in Spain. In this way, Mendes opened an escape route for all those fleeing the Nazis. These included Jews and gentiles—artists, writers, even royalty. Mendes knew he was taking a great risk. He also knew that if he couldn't get the Jews out of France, they would surely be deported to concentration camps and eventually die. Over thirty thousand Jews entered Portugal with his visas in hand. The Portuguese government was furious and demanded that Mendes stop issuing them, but he continued to defy these orders. He was dismissed from his post but secretly still issued visas bearing his signature.

Mendes was ordered by his government to leave France at once and return to Portugal. When the diplomat arrived home, Antonio Salazar, Portugal's premier, wanted to put him on trial for insubordination. The thousands of refugees in Portugal whom he had saved, including many of the royalty, openly voiced their opposition. Salazar was afraid of all this bad publicity and backed down. The world learned of Mendes's deeds and praised Portugal as a haven for refugees. Salazar shrewdly took all the credit for Mendes's work. He loved this good publicity his country was receiving and said it was his idea to issue the visas.

As fate would have it, this Portuguese dictator decided to follow Mendes's humanitarian example and kept his borders open to all refugees who managed to escape. He persuaded Spain to do the same, but he never forgave Mendes. He banished him from the foreign service. Mendes's own country shunned him and trampled on his good name. Unable to get a job, he had to feed his family at a soup kitchen run by the Hebrew Immigrant Society. He was forced to live in poverty and disgrace.

His wife became sickly from malnutrition and died. Six years after her death, Mendes also died, broken, alone, and forgotten. He had hoped that his government would clear his name and restore his honor while he was still alive. That never happened.

Knowing what he did to help thousands of Jews, the Hebrew Immigrant Society helped his children emigrate to various countries, including the United States.

Today, a memorial to Aristides de Sousa Mendes stands outside his old decaying home in Portugal. The villagers take great pride in their local hero and maintain this memorial. He paid a great personal price for his heroism, and many, many Jews owe their lives to this Righteous Gentile. The State of Israel recognized this great diplomat as "Righteous Among the Nations" and planted a tree in his honor at Yad Vashem. There he takes his rightful place alongside Raoul Wallenberg, Per Anger, Carl Lutz, and Senpo Sugihara. He will always be honored by the survivors and their children for his bravery.

Toby's thoughts were suddenly interrupted by her teacher. "Come on, girls. The bus will be leaving in a few minutes and you have to finish up."

As Toby reluctantly prepared to leave the Hall of Names, she knew that someday she would return to Yad Vashem and learn more about these Righteous Gentiles. "Goodbye, my heroes," she whispered, as she and Donna left the hall. "And thank you."

On the return trip to the hotel, there was none of the usual joking or singing on the bus. The class knew they would be returning home tomorrow, but they would always remember the day they visited Yad Vashem and learned about the heroes and martyrs memorialized there.

PART 6

Back Home in Louisiana

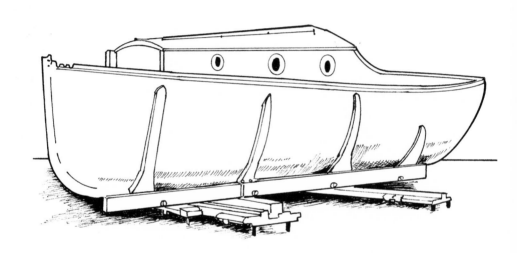

CHAPTER 28

Toby Tells All about Her Trip

When Toby arrived back home in Louisiana, everyone was anxious to hear about her trip. The following day, the family gathered around the breakfast table and listened as Toby read from her travel journal.

Toby had written everything down. She did not want to forget the wonderful sights she saw and the different foods she tasted. But the highlight for her was her trip to Yad Vashem. "Did you know that Yad Vashem means 'hand of God' in Hebrew?" she asked. Toby told her parents about the Righteous Gentiles and the trees and plaques with the names of the men and women honored by Israel for their heroic deeds. "They were all Christians," she said. "I even spent time reading some awesome stories about them and how they saved so many Jewish lives." She thought back to the Hall of Names.

Mr. Belfer had an idea. "Toby, why don't you tell their stories at our Friday evening Shabbat service at temple?"

"Oh, that's a great idea, Papa! Maybe I'll ask the rabbi if he could invite some of our Christian friends to the service. I'm sure they would be pleased to hear about these gentile heroes."

The following Friday evening, some special guests were present for the service at the Belfers' synagogue. Father O'Connor from Donna's Catholic church and Pastor Goodby from the big Baptist church were in attendance. As part of the service, Toby nervously told the congregation about her trip to Yad Vashem and how she learned about the Righteous Gentiles. As she gave examples of their bravery, not another sound was heard in the sanctuary. All attention was focused on her.

After the service, a reception was held in the social hall. Coffee, tea, and Mama's homemade apple and pecan pies were served, along with punch for the children. Everyone came up to congratulate Toby about her talk. Kids her age said they learned a lot from her stories. Father O'Connor and Pastor Goodby asked Toby if she would like to tell about her trip in their Sunday-school classes. "I'm certain our students would be interested in learning about these people who helped the Jews," said the pastor. Father O'Connor readily agreed.

Toby was flattered and excited that she was asked to do this. "I would like the whole world to know about these brave people," she said and agreed to tell her stories at their churches.

When they returned home from the synagogue, Mama told Toby she was very proud of her. "You know," she added, "there are some Righteous Gentiles right here in the South."

"There are? Who are they, and where are they from, Mama?" asked Toby, with a puzzled look on her face.

"In Whitwell, Tennessee," Mama replied. She told Toby about the wonderful people in that small community who built the "Paper Clip" Children's Museum.

"Oh, Mama, can we go and see them?" asked an excited Toby.

"Perhaps over Labor Day weekend," answered her mother.

CHAPTER 29

Toby Learns about More
Righteous Gentiles

Toby spent much of her spare time during summer break in the library learning everything she could about those who helped Jews survive the Holocaust. She knew that there were over twenty thousand heroes honored at Yad Vashem as Righteous Gentiles. She saw many trees planted in their honor and their names inscribed on the Wall of Heroes. But she also knew that hundreds of other good Christians helped Jews survive and their names are unknown. None of them expected rewards or honors. They did what they did because it was the right thing to do.

"Toby, you are spending so much time in the library this summer," Mama noted, somewhat concerned. "You look pale!"

"But I'm learning lots of things," Toby replied. "Did you know that most of Italy's Jews were rescued by Catholic clergymen? I read that lots of priests, monks, and nuns sheltered Jewish men, women, and children in their churches, monasteries, and convents."

It's true that many priests and bishops put their lives in jeopardy to hide Jews from the Nazis. They gave them shelter, food, and clothing. Not many other countries like Italy opened their religious institutions to Jews. These brave people expected nothing in return and even allowed the Jews to hold services on the Sabbath. Hiding these poor refugees saved thousands of lives. One of Toby's fifth-grade teachers was Italian, and Toby was going to tell him what she just learned.

The next time Toby went to the library, she read about Denmark. She found out that, of all the countries the Nazis occupied, only Denmark rescued most of its entire Jewish population. The Jews in Denmark were considered Danes first and foremost. They were accepted and respected as friends, neighbors, and good citizens. When the Germans occupied their little country in 1940, the Danes were allowed to run their own affairs for a while and Danish Jews were left alone. Like the rest of the population, the Jews went about their business, though always keeping a watchful eye on their Nazi occupiers. They heard about the terrible things happening to Jews elsewhere.

Things changed for the worse in 1943. A friendly German diplomat warned Danish leaders that their Jews were going to be rounded up and transported to concentration camps. The Danish response was swift. They organized a nationwide effort to smuggle their Jews to Sweden.

First they found hiding places for their Jewish friends and neighbors in homes, churches, and hospitals. Then they rounded up enough fishermen and their boats to ferry the Jews across the narrow water that separated Denmark from Sweden. This was a very dangerous trip because German boats constantly patrolled these waters. Over seven thousand Danish Jews were transported in these tiny wooden fishing boats. The boats made several trips, because they could only smuggle up to fourteen at a time. Many families separated, leaving mothers and fathers behind while their children went on the boats. Most reunited in Sweden, but some did not. The nationwide effort proved that resistance to Nazi policies and support for Jews could indeed save many lives.

"What wonderful people those heroic Danes were," Toby thought to herself. "I can't wait to tell Mama and Papa about them."

During her research, Toby also became aware of the important role the Society of Friends, or Quakers, played in helping Jews escape from the Nazis. She didn't know much about this religious sect except what she learned in her history class. She remembered that the Quakers founded Rhode Island to escape the religious persecution of the Puritans. "Just like the Jews," Toby thought.

It was interesting to read that the Society of Friends and the Jehovah's Witnesses were the only religious groups that adopted a formal policy of helping Jews. She decided to learn more about it. She studied several books in the library and found out that the Quakers were always ready to offer aid to anyone in need. When they saw what was happening to the Jewish population in Germany, they raised money to help these people emigrate to other countries before they were deported to concentration camps. They also established a service to care for children whose parents had been imprisoned. They sent them to foster parents in England and paid for their upkeep. The Quakers were allowed to enter some of the concentration camps and provide food and medical supplies to all who were imprisoned. They saw firsthand the horrible conditions in these camps. In 1949, the American Society of Friends was awarded the Nobel Peace prize for their service to humanity.

When the war ended, the Quakers went to rebuild European cities that had been devastated by bombs. This concept helped establish the Peace Corps in the United States. "Maybe someday Donna and I will join the Peace Corps," Toby thought. "I would like to follow the example of the Quakers and help others."

There were many individual Quakers who, at great risk to themselves, helped Jews escape from the Nazis. Many of them are honored at Yad Vashem, and Toby remembered reading about one, Elisabeth Abegg.

Toby was in the library most days during the summer recess. She read stories of other Christians who helped Jews during the war. They may not have their names on the wall at Yad Vashem, but they will surely be remembered for their bravery. One such story she read was about a young boy in Poland.

His name was Harry, and he was only eight years old when he watched from a hiding place as his parents were killed by the Germans. When the soldiers left, he crawled through a fence and walked through the woods. After walking all night, he finally saw a light in the distance. Harry didn't know what it was, but he kept heading towards it. As he approached, he saw that the light came from a small farmhouse. Cold, starving, and desperate, he crawled up to the house and knocked on the door. Someone inside said in a voice loud enough for him to hear, "Don't open the door." Then he heard a woman's voice saying, "But it might be someone who needs help."

The door slowly opened, and a woman appeared. She stared at the cold and trembling boy on her doorstep. This kind stranger pulled Harry inside the warm house and sat him by the fire. She wrapped him in a woolen blanket and fed him some hot soup. She asked him his name and heard the story about his mother and father. He said he was Jewish, but she took him in and hid him in her attic. She kept Harry safe until the end of the war. She never told him her name. But she was his hero, and he would never forget this kindly stranger who saved his life. She was certainly a Righteous Gentile.

Marlena lived in Berlin. It was 1939, and Jews all over Germany were being persecuted, beaten, and even imprisoned. Marlena's father asked her if she would like to go on a train ride. Of course she would, for she had never been on a train before. The train went to Belgium, and when they got off, a kindly lady was waiting for them. She took Marlena by the hand and started to walk away. To the child's surprise and puzzlement, her father got back on the train and left for home. That was the last time Marlena saw him or her mother. The Belgian lady became her foster parent. When the Germans invaded Belgium, Marlena's foster parent hid the Jewish child in a large dresser drawer. The drawer actually became Marlena's home. When she outgrew it, she was hidden in the outhouse in the backyard. The child was fed bread and soup once a day and stayed in that hiding place until the war ended. This kind Belgian lady never told Marlena her name. She had simply said, "Call me *Oma*" ("Grandmother"). "Oma" was one of the hundreds of non-Jews who risked their lives to save Jewish children during the war.

In Bulgaria, the Germans had sent Leah Farchi's husband to a labor camp while she was pregnant. When it came time for this young Jewish woman to have her baby, she had no place to go. Jews were not permitted to go to a hospital in Bulgaria. In desperation, she turned to her friend Stanka Stoicheva ("Stoy-*shay*-vah") for help. Her friend was a midwife, or a woman who helps deliver babies, and she told Leah to come to her house. She delivered Leah's baby, and both Leah and her baby remained hidden in Stanka's attic. They were fed, clothed, and sheltered until the end of the war. This Righteous Gentile saved two Jewish lives.

Toby was surprised to learn that Bulgaria protested so strongly against the deportation of their Jewish citizens that the Germans finally gave in and stopped. Even though Bulgaria was an ally of Germany, they felt that their Jews were Bulgarians first and must be protected. This was in contrast to other allies of Germany such as Vichy France and Hungary. The Jews in Bulgaria had the king and the Bulgarian Orthodox Church make sure their Jewish citizens were safe. How do you thank all of these nameless heroes for saving so many lives?

Toby read and absorbed as much as she could, but summer recess was drawing to a close. She wanted to ask Mama about her promised trip to Tennessee, so she could learn more about the Righteous Gentiles in the South.

PART 7

Visit to Whitwell, Tennessee

CHAPTER 30

Toby Tours the "Paper Clip" Children's Museum

The Belfers and Donna finalized their plans to visit Whitwell, Tennessee, where the children's Holocaust museum was located. They all piled into Mr. Belfer's van and left on Labor Day weekend.

It was a long ride from Louisiana, but everyone was excited about the trip. They finally arrived in this small Tennessee community exhausted but happy. Labor Day in Whitwell was a day of parades, entertainment, good Southern cooking, and fun for the entire family. The Belfers looked forward to introducing themselves to Linda Hooper, the principal of Whitwell Middle School, where the "Paper Clip Project" originated.

When they met Ms. Hooper, she told them that requests for guided tours of the museum have to be made in advance. However, when she learned about Toby and Donna's trip to Israel, she agreed to give them a personal tour, even though the museum is closed on Labor Day. She was impressed with these two eleven-year-old girls from Louisiana.

As they began to tour the museum, Ms. Hooper told them that the "Paper Clip Project" started in 1998 with a simple but profound idea: "the feelings that connect us are greater than those that divide us." The results of the project were amazing. A memorial railcar with 11 million paper clips in a glass case stands permanently in the schoolyard. These represent the 6 million Jews and 5 million others killed by the Nazis. This little railcar teaches an unforgettable lesson of how a committed group of people in a small Southern town "changed the world, one classroom at a time."

The project began when the eighth-grade students at Whitwell Middle School were first introduced to the study of the Holocaust. Their teacher, Sandra Roberts, suggested that they use this study to strive for individual tolerance. The class of 425 had no Jewish students. The lesson began with the fact that 6 million Jews were killed by the Germans during World War II. Most of European Jewry was wiped out by these planned killings.

One student remarked that he couldn't imagine what 6 million of anything looked like. Another student asked if they could collect 6 million of something so that they could see. He was told yes, but it had to be connected to the Holocaust in some way.

After many hours of research, they discovered that the paper clip, invented by a Norwegian in 1899, was worn by Norwegians during World War II to protest the Nazis' policies when their country was occupied by Germany. The paper clip became a symbol of solidarity against the Nazi racist policies.

The students set about publicizing their request for paper clips. People all over the world learned about their project from newspaper articles, the Internet, and word of mouth. Before long, paper clips by the dozens, and then the thousands, began pouring into Whitwell, Tennessee. Amazingly, the students eventually collected over 30 million paper clips.

Ms. Hooper wanted to put the clips in an authentic transport car that had taken Jews to the concentration camps. But where would she find one? The principal enlisted the aid of two German journalists who were working in the United States. Peter and Dagmar Schroeder traveled all over Europe until they finally found an original car in a railroad museum near Berlin, Germany. The car was built in 1917 and was used to transport Jews to the camps. After the war, it served as a grain car until it was retired and sent to the museum. The Schroeders had this car shipped through the port of Baltimore and then transported to Tennessee. On October 5, 2001, three years after the "Paper Clip Project" originated, it arrived in Whitwell.

As Toby and her group strolled along the path in the museum's garden, they noticed eighteen butterflies, some sculpted of twisted copper and some hand painted, embedded in the concrete. Ms. Hooper explained that the idea of the butterflies came from the book *I Never Saw Another Butterfly*, which is a collection of works by the children at the Terezin concentration camp. In this camp where so many children were imprisoned and died, they wrote poetry and stories and drew pictures. These works were about hope, life, and freedom. Butterflies represented the freedom they all sought.

"Oh, I remember seeing many of those butterfly drawings at Yad Vashem last spring!" Toby exclaimed. "I know the children who drew them only wanted to be as free as butterflies," she sadly recalled. She also explained to Donna, "In Hebrew, the number eighteen is called *chai,* which also means 'life,' so I think the eighteen butterflies is really a neat idea."

Inside the railroad car, besides the 11 million paper clips are books and mementos. There is also a suitcase donated by a German school that contains letters of apology to Anne Frank. These German children also studied the Holocaust and were ashamed of this terrible event. They wanted to express their regrets and chose to write these letters. A sculpture by a Tennessee artist stands in the garden as a memorial to the victims of the Holocaust. The sculpture incorporates 11 million more paper clips.

Holocaust survivors visit the museum periodically. They share their experiences during the war with the students and with this wonderful community who volunteered their time and effort to build the museum. The survivors make presentations at the local church and are grateful for the opportunity to talk to the students, their parents, and members of the community. They insist that "the museum is not a symbol of tragedy, but a project of hope and inspiration."

At the conclusion of the tour, Toby said to her parents, "What a glorious way to end a fabulous summer. I think we should plant a tree at Yad Vashem to honor the Righteous Gentiles of Whitwell, Tennessee." Toby thanked Ms. Hooper for the tour. She added, "Now I know the true meaning of heroes and martyrs. The martyrs are the 6 million Jews who died in the Holocaust, never losing pride in their faith and religion. The 21,000 people recognized as 'Righteous Among the Nations' are the heroes."

"Don't forget all those Christians whose names will never be known but saved many Jews," said Donna.

"Yes," replied Toby, "heroes for sure."

On the way home to Louisiana, everyone proudly wore a paper clip on their clothing. Toby thought back to Anne Frank's diary and repeated softly to herself her famous words. *"Despite everything, I believe people are really good at heart."*

Afterword

Toby Belfer, our fictional eleven-year-old Jewish girl, lives in the South among her Christian friends and neighbors. She goes to school with them, plays with them, shops with them, and is free to practice her religious faith.

This was not so for people like Toby during World War II in Europe. Even though people of the Jewish faith have been subjected to cruel persecution throughout history, nothing like what happened to them in Germany and the rest of occupied Europe could ever have been imagined. Over 6 million Jews were killed by the Nazis in what they called "the Final Solution." Today, this terrible tragedy is known as the Holocaust and is studied in schools throughout the world. Many thousands of Jewish lives were saved by Christians in every country that was occupied by the Germans during that period.

The Museum for the Remembrance of Holocaust Martyrs and Heroes in Jerusalem, known as Yad Vashem, honors more than twenty thousand of these Righteous Gentiles. Many more of these noble Christians will never be honored by name because they are unknown. They did not peform these heroic deeds looking for rewards. They did them simply because it was the right and moral thing to do.

The survivors of Nazi concentration camps are now quite old. Many have already died. The remaining survivors tell their stories in order to educate young people about the horror that took place many years ago. It is important for the children of today to hear these stories, so they can grow up to be the righteous people of tomorrow.

Toby Belfer and her friend Donna will never forget their visits to Yad Vashem and Whitwell, Tennessee. They read about the courage of the Jewish martyrs and of the heroes recognized as "Righteous Among the Nations." How do you thank these heroes and martyrs for their bravery? Embrace their values as you grow up.

Glossary

anti-Semitism: A form of hostility, prejudice, and discrimination directed towards persons of the Jewish faith. Adolf Hitler practiced violent anti-Semitism in Germany and the occupied countries during World War II.

concentration camps: Places where Jews and others opposed to the Nazi regime were imprisoned. Many died of starvation and disease; others were killed by the Nazis.

diplomat: An individual appointed to represent his or her government in relation to another government and live in that country. The United States has diplomats called ambassadors in foreign countries. Consuls work for the ambassadors and are also considered diplomats.

Dome of the Rock: One of Islam's holiest sites. It is located in Jerusalem.

embassy: An official government building in the capital of a foreign country where the ambassador lives and works. An embassy is considered part of the country it represents. The U.S. has embassies in almost every foreign country it has good relations with, and the embassies are respected as American territory.

eternal flame: A fire that never goes out and is a memorial to remember some important person or a group of heroic people no longer living. Pres. John F. Kennedy has an eternal flame burning at his gravesite in Arlington National Cemetery. The 6 million Jews killed in the Holocaust have an eternal flame burning in their memory at Yad Vashem.

Final Solution: A Nazi program aimed at exterminating all the Jews in Europe.

gentile: A person not of the Jewish faith, usually a Christian.

Gestapo: The German secret police who carried out all of Hitler's policies. They were often violent and brutal in their methods.

ghetto: A walled-off section of a city where the Nazis forced Jews to live, separate from the rest of the population. The Germans set up ghettos in most major cities they occupied. The living conditions were terrible and many died from starvation or disease. The Warsaw ghetto in Poland is famous for the rebellion of the Jews living there. Beginning in April 1943, with hardly any guns or ammunition, the Jews rose up and fought the mighty German army for a month. Of the 400,000 Jews originally in the ghetto, only 38,000 were alive when the German army destroyed the ghetto with their tanks and artillery. The remainder were either imprisoned or shot. These heroic Jews are remembered at Yad Vashem.

hero: A person admired for his or her bravery and extraordinary deeds. The Righteous Gentiles who aided the Jews were heroes.

Hitler, Adolf: The political leader of Germany from 1933 to 1945. He was one of the most brutal dictators in history. He started World War II and was responsible for the destruction of most of Europe and the deaths of 6 million Jews and countless others who opposed his policies. He was generally thought to be mad and committed suicide in a secret bunker in Berlin as the Soviet army was approaching the city.

Holocaust: The term used to describe the Nazi murder of 6 million Jews in Europe. It was one of the most horrible events in history.

Kaddish: The Jewish prayer for the dead recited at funerals and on the anniversary of the individual's death. The prayer sanctifies God and life.

martyr: A person who chooses to suffer or die rather than give up his or her faith or beliefs. Jesus Christ was considered a martyr, as were the Jews killed by the Nazis.

Nazi: An individual who belonged to Hitler's political party. The majority of Germans, especially military and government officials, were Nazis during World War II, but some Germans opposed Hitler. Many Nazis were brutal and violent in carrying out Hitler's policies. Those in Germany who weren't Nazis were considered traitors.

neutral country: A country that takes no side in a war and hopes to avoid being attacked by the warring countries. Sweden, Switzerland, Spain, and Portugal were neutral countries during the Second World War. Many Jews, fearing for their lives, tried to flee to those nations to escape the Nazis.

visa: An official authorization from a country permitting entry and travel within that country. Jews needed visas to escape to neutral countries. Embassies and consulates were authorized to issue visas. Many foreign diplomats such as Sugihara and Mendes defied their governments' orders and issued visas to Jews, permitting them to flee the Nazis.

World War II: A war fought from 1939 to 1945 by Great Britain, France, the Soviet Union, the United States, and others against Germany, Italy, and Japan. Italy changed sides in 1943. Germany was finally defeated in May 1945, and Japan surrendered in September 1945. This war was one of the most destructive in history and changed the entire landscape of Europe and Japan. Over 60 million soldiers and civilians were killed. Many German military men were punished for war crimes they committed, and Germany was divided into four zones, with the United States, Great Britain, France, and the Soviet Union each controlling a zone. Japan was occupied by the United States. Today, Germany and Japan are both democratic nations and are friends and allies of the United States. We hope we never see another world war.

Sources

City University of New York, Holocaust Research Center and Archives.

Frank, Anne. *The Diary of a Young Girl.* 1947. Reprint, New York: Bantam Books, 1993.

Halter, Marek. *Stories of Deliverance.* Chicago: Open Court, 1998.

The Holocaust Chronicle: A History in Words and Pictures. Lindenwood, N.J.: Publications International, 2001.

Jewish Virtual Library (Internet research library; biographies of Righteous Gentiles). www.jewishvirtuallibrary.org.

Meltzer, Milton. *Rescue: How Gentiles Saved Jews in the Holocaust.* New York: Harper and Row, 1988.

The Museum of Tolerance, Los Angeles, Calif., Documents and Archives Center

Paper Clip Project. Production of the Johnson Group in association with Miramax Films and Ergo Entertainment, 2006. Documentary.

Tulane University Research Library, New Orleans, La., Documents and Archives Section.

Yad Vashem, Jerusalem, Israel, Righteous Gentiles Archives.